DOCTOR FROWNYFACE PRESENTS

BONETINGLERS

by Dusty Trice

ISBN Paperback: 979-8-9850737-4-4

Ebook: 979-8-9850737-5-1

Library of Congress Control Number: 2023945150

First paperback edition September 18, 2023.

Cover Art and Illustrations by Dusty Trice
Edited by Shelea Van Hoose
Book Layout by www.fiverr.com/sarco2000

Read-O-Vision LLC, A Publishing Company
6450 Sunset Blvd. #1107, Hollywood, CA 90028
ReadOVision.com

CHEAP
PLASTIC
SKELETONS
FROM
HELL

INTRODUCTION

The terrifying tale contained in this book will rock you, shock you, and tingle your bones!

Just kidding, this book is stupid. This book should never have been made and someone should have stopped the author from completing it. The publisher should feel tremendous shame for agreeing to print and present such a stupid book to a mature reading public. I feel stupider now having read this incredibly, ridiculously, unfathomably stupid book. And now so can you!

Hello, my name is Doctor Frownyface and I'm a book presenter.

As a mad scientist and lover of all things spooky, I must object to the truly lighthearted, dare I say jokey, tone of this book. A proper horror novelette should be packed to the gills with long, drawn out poetic descriptions of splatter and gore, not simple minded slapstick, dumb puns, and fart jokes.

I expect the horror literature I read to make my skin crawl until I must put it down in disgust, not thrill and tantalize me with funny dialogue and creepy themes like some sort of brainless entertainment.

Good horror literature should at least have zombies, a sexy werewolf, or maybe a creepy doll. This book has none of that and goes for lowbrow laughs by putting cheap plastic skeletons in Halloween costumes and making them move around.

Even the ending was bad. Seriously, fuck everyone involved with this book... Oh. Wait. So, I WASN'T supposed to be reviewing this book? The publisher just wanted me to write a nice introduction? Right. And their check cleared? Well, in that case...

Grab a drink and make yourself comfortable on the couch, chair, or toilet where you do most of your reading, and get ready to spend the next couple of hours laughing the shit out of yourself while wishing you had chosen to read a different book.

Make better choices next time,

Doctor Frownyface
Mad Scientist/Horror Book Presenter

DBNR

CHAPTER 1

The industrial plastic mixing vat at the center of the factory floor simmered and stirred its creamy white petrochemical contents in a steady swirl. The enormous cauldron of cheap molten plastic, favored by the High Quality Novelty Company, bubbled with noxious orange vapors that drifted up toward the corrugated metal ceiling of the factory. There the lingering fumes were sucked out into the stale evening air by giant exhaust fans to join the other lingering fumes that hung like an opaque fog over Shenzhen City in the Guangdong Province of China.

Manufacturing foreman Factory King, Wáng Gōngchǎng, paced the aisles of the sweltering hot shop and smoked a cigarette as he smoothed the tendrils of greasy hair that clung to his sweaty forehead. He stopped briefly to inspect the work of the tiny hands that assembled the cheap plastic skeletons and other Halloween decorations on their little metal workbenches, which were spaced tightly along the walls of the grimy factory.

"Work faster, slugs!" Factory King shouted at the children in Chinese as he flattened his combover with a dirty palm.

A small shoeless boy in grubby red overalls, exhausted from the heat, dabbed the sweat from his eyes and momentarily laid his head down on his workbench. It did not go unnoticed. Factory King was watching. The children knew he was always watching.

"You have time to sleep on my factory line? I suppose you also have time to sleep… on the streets!" Factory King snarled as he kicked the little stool out from under the resting boy.

The stool clattered across the factory floor and hit another little boy wearing a stained, green-striped shirt in the hip as he painted brown grit on a pile of plastic skeleton femurs. The boy in the red overalls fell backwards into a dark, murky puddle of water on the filthy floor as Factory King loomed over him and laughed.

"Heh heh heh, ha ha ha!"

The boy in the green-striped shirt fought back tears as he rubbed his bruised hip in the spot the stool had struck him. Then he picked up the stool and ran it back across the factory to where it belonged, pausing briefly to help the boy in the red overalls to his feet, before he headed back to his own workbench.

"You!" bellowed Factory King as he seized the boy in the green-striped shirt by the collar and yanked him from his stool. "Did I say you should leave your position on the line?"

The terrified little boy silently shook his head no. Factory King lifted the boy off the floor, stretching his green-striped shirt, and brought the child within inches of his smokey, unshaven face. Factory King turned to inspect the boy's workstation. His eyes narrowed.

"Do you call this painting adequate?" barked Factory King as he hauled the dangling boy before the pile of painted plastic femurs. "Answer me, worm!"

"No, sir," sobbed the boy in Chinese. "I'm so sorry, Factory King. It will never happen again, sir."

"Paint better. Now!" Factory King screamed and spat in the child's face before he threw him down onto his stool like a rag doll. "And paint faster, you little shit! Heh heh heh, ha ha ha!"

The boy in the green-striped shirt grabbed his paintbrush and began to splash brown paint on the plastic femurs at a frantic pace. The rest of the factory children cowered in fear as Factory King stalked across the floor, puffed his cigarette, and laughed menacingly at them as he eyeballed their work.

A small sob came from behind a pile of plastic skulls near the end of the assembly line. Factory King wheeled around and stomped toward the source of the crying. A young girl in an aqua blue dress with a bright pink bow in her hair stood between a bin of headless plastic skeleton torsos and a big pile of plastic skeleton skulls. Tears rolled down her soot-stained cheeks. Factory King noticed a plastic skeleton with its head on backwards lying on the girl's workbench.

"You stupid clown," Factory King said as he snatched the plastic skeleton from the bench and shoved it into the little girl's face. "Does that look right to you, clown?"

The little girl balled up her fists and raised them to her eyes as she sobbed and shook uncontrollably.

"I want my mommy," the little girl cried.

"Do you want your mommy now, little clown? You are such a little clown; I wonder if your mommy even still wants you?" Factory King roared as he twisted the skull of the plastic skeleton the right way around. "Get your head on straight. Less crying and more making plastic skeletons or you'll end up like the last little girl who cried in my factory. Do you know what happened to her, little clown?"

The little girl wiped her eyes on the sleeve of her dirty aqua dress and shook her head no.

"She died of shame, and I used her bones to make the mold for the skeleton you are assembling," Factory King said. The little girl screamed and ran crying toward the employee door. "Do better tomorrow or don't bother coming back, little clown. Heh heh heh, ha ha ha!"

The children all knew this was no idle threat. Factory King controlled everything in their little world. He had purchased the children from their poor, rural parents. Parents who in most cases were actually happy to take his money and have one less mouth to feed. Parents who believed, deep in their hearts, that anything would be better for their children than a future of sickness, fieldwork, and early death.

Factory King promised to pay the children, feed and care for them, and give them lodging. And Factory King paid the parents well, which somehow, in their eyes, made him more trustworthy. And Factory King was a man of his word.

He did house the children, eight to a room in a windowless dormitory-style tenement. He did feed the children, rice and meat from mongrel dogs that he shot in the alleyways behind the factory. He did pay a man to delouse the children quarterly and give them antibiotics when they were sick or injured, which was often.

The children worked in his factory for 80-120 hours a week, depending on the size of Halloween decoration orders from the American retailers. And after Factory King had deducted the cost of what little he did do for the children from their meager pay, he gave them each only a few cents an hour for their work. And they took their slave wages gratefully, buying sweets and clothes, because they were only little children who knew nothing else but a life of hard work in a toxic factory, sickness, and suffering.

Factory King looked up at the nicotine stained, metal-caged clock that hung above his metal-caged office, grabbed the pull chain to the end-of-day whistle, and gave it a firm tug. The shrill blast of the steam whistle echoed through the factory as the children set down their tools and plastic bones and leapt from their tiny stools.

"Get out of here, you worthless brats!" hollered Factory King, flicking his cigarette toward the children as they bolted for the employee door.

The sky had turned gray, and drizzle fell in sheets as the children opened the factory door and ran outside to their dormitory. Factory King walked to the open door, saw the little girl in the aqua dress and pink bow standing barefoot in a puddle outside, quaking as she sobbed uncontrollably, and then smirked at her as he slammed the employee door closed.

"Heh heh heh, ha ha ha!"

CHAPTER 2

A violent storm raged outside the metal walls of the factory. Lightning illuminated the deep wrinkles on the face of Factory King as he sat behind the beat up green iron desk in his cramped factory office, where he listened to the radio and checked company emails on an ancient desktop computer. He looked away from the screen briefly to glare at a gigantic skeleton hand prototype sitting amongst the mountain of papers on his desk.

Factory King noshed on a big bowl of dog meat and rice, shoved the prototype aside, then emptied a clear glass of sauce baijiu down his throat. He unbuttoned the front of his sweat-yellowed shirt, lit a fresh cigarette from the one he was smoking, and stared at a list of new Halloween decoration purchase order emails coming in from the American retailers. Americans sure loved their Halloween decorations, and Factory King loved purchase order emails from American retailers.

The night was cold and rainy, but the cheap molten plastic that perpetually mixed in the big vat kept the factory hot and steamy. Factory King wiped his brow and stumbled drunkenly to the gross little fridge where he kept his supply of snacks and liquor. He poured himself another glass of baijiu and wiped his greasy comb-over back into place on his balding scalp.

Something crashed to the floor in the darkness outside his office. Factory King looked out through the blinds and scowled as a flash of lightning filled the factory floor in flickering light.

"Fucking rodents," Factory King muttered to himself, stubbed out his cigarette in the ashtray on his desk, and turned up the volume on the radio. He cradled his drink as he sloshed to the door and grabbed the crowbar he kept propped against the door jam. He threw open his office door and pounded out onto the factory floor. A fresh wave of plastic fumes stabbed him in the sinuses.

"Hey, you stupid rats! You might as well call it a night, huh? There's none of those peasant kids here for you to eat this late in the night. Stupids!" Factory King yelled, then laughed as he stumbled around the floor and battered a cardboard box loudly with his crowbar. "Heh heh heh, ha ha… ha. If I catch you, I'm going to crush your little rat skulls, you bastards. You fucking hear me?"

Something rustled in the darkness of the factory and Factory King wheeled around, ready to attack. Brownish spit glazed his teeth as his lips parted into a wicked grin.

Factory King patted the crowbar against the side of his calf, took a sip of his drink, and hummed along to the music on the radio that blared from his office. A clang, like a lead pipe falling, came from the metal catwalk high above the mixing machine and big vat of cheap molten plastic.

"Now I've got you, stupids," Factory King spat through wet lips.

He stumbled to the ladder leading up to the catwalk and slowly began to climb, drink and crowbar still in hand. He momentarily lost his grip halfway up, caught himself, secured the crowbar in his armpit, took a sip of his drink, then continued slowly climbing the ladder.

A red-faced Factory King reached up and carefully placed the crowbar and his drink tumbler on the catwalk and grunted as he pulled himself the rest of the way up. He gave a long middle-aged groan as he bent over to pick up his drink. Wobbling, he put the crowbar back under his arm, spit in his hand to fix his combover with his palm, and loudly slurped from his drink.

"Come out, come out, wherever you are," Factory King slurred as he took another sip of baijiu. A loud, hollow thump echoed ahead of him on the dark catwalk. A dirty box of defective plastic skeleton pieces had fallen from behind a storage rack. Brittle and bent bones rained down onto the factory floor beside the mixing vat. Factory King's eyes darted to the shadows moving behind the rack and his grin widened.

"There you are, you stupid fucking fuckers," he growled as he pulled his arm back and threw his empty drink glass into the darkness near the rack. The glass tumbler sailed through the air and shattered on a child's workbench below. He laughed as he stumbled along the shadowy catwalk toward the source of the sounds. "Heh heh heh, ha ha ha."

The greasy foreman ran his hand along the shaky safety rail to steady himself as he crept across the rickety metal catwalk, clutching the crowbar in his other hand. Factory King ground his nasty, rotten teeth together and swung the crowbar hard into the railing. The brutal clang of metal striking metal reverberated throughout the factory. Orangish steam escaped from bubbles in the molten plastic below and rose through the open metal grating of the catwalk as he made his way over the top of the enormous churning vat. He raised the crowbar high over his head as he rounded the corner leading to the storage rack.

Factory King had no time to react as the three small children put their momentum behind the heavy metal hook suspended from a long chain that hung from the ceiling. The little girl in the aqua dress and pink bow gave a tiny battle cry as she and the boy in the red overalls and the boy in the green-striped shirt shoved the metal hook directly at the evil factory foreman.

The metal hook struck Factory King hard in the chest. Factory King screamed and watched as the hook pierced his pectoral muscle and lodged between his ribs. Blood gushed from Factory King's chest as he stumbled backwards and slammed into the catwalk railing, a railing he had improperly installed himself, which promptly gave way in a very, very unsafe manner.

Factory King lurched backwards and pinwheeled his arms in vain in an attempt to maintain his balance. The crowbar flew out of his hand and clattered loudly into the control panel of the plastic mixer below. The massive machine's paddles spun into high gear. The thick molten plastic began to slosh and froth as the paddles whirled, faster and faster.

"Children, please," begged Factory King, too drunk

to steady himself as he reached out to the little girl. "Help me!"

The little girl in the aqua dress and pink bow gave another little battle cry as she ran forward, shoved Factory King, and sent him sailing over the catwalk railing. The slack went out of the chain suspended from the ceiling as the giant metal hook bit deeply into Factory King's chest. His ribs crackled and snapped as he swung out over the plastic vat.

"Help me!" Factory King screamed through a mouthful of blood as he looked down in total terror at the bloody hook embedded in his chest.

The children stepped to the edge of the catwalk and looked down to where Factory King dangled. The little girl in the aqua dress and pink bow held a controller in her hand.

The little girl pressed the button on the controller. The chain hanging from the ceiling began to lower Factory King down into the plastic vat.

"No. No!!! NOOOO!!!!!" Factory King pleaded as he sunk into the hot plastic. "AAAaaahhhhh!!!!!"

Factory King howled in pain as the mixer paddles shattered his ankles. His skin burned as he was swept deeper into the plastic mixer. Factory King's eyes, ears, nose, and mouth filled with molten plastic as he desperately reached up with both hands to where the children silently watched him from the catwalk.

A big bolt of lightning flashed in the stormy night sky and illuminated the large basin of scalding, liquified plastic. Factory King screamed his last living breath and thrashed as the speeding mixer pulled his broken and quivering body beneath the surface.

The thick white plastic began to swirl red with blood as the mixer mangled and crushed his corpse in the bottom of the big vat. The children quickly climbed down the ladder from the catwalk with satisfied, but scared, looks on their little faces.

Another bolt of lightning shot from the sky and struck the factory roof with a gigantic crack. A bluish green glow filled the factory floor as electricity sizzled down from the chain that hung from the ceiling. Daggers of green lightning arched toward the vat of molten plastic and a deep laugh came from somewhere within the mixing machine. A sudden wind swirled within the factory and sent loose papers and wrappers dancing throughout the air.

"Heh heh heh, ha ha ha!"

The three little children screamed and huddled together as bolts of green lightning zapped the catwalk above them.

"Heh heh heh, ha ha ha!"

Glowing green plastic charged with electricity as it poured through big tubes that led from the vat to mold machines around the factory floor. The gooey plastic crackled as it oozed into the bone molds, where it was transformed into luminous plastic parts for cheap plastic skeletons.

"HEH HEH HEH, HA HA HA!!!"

All that remained of Factory King's physical form were the flecks of blood, guts, and bone that speckled the glowing hard plastic pieces dropping from the molding machines into big bins by each little factory workbench.

The lightning fizzled into green sparks and Factory King's laughter died away to silence. A gentle rain pitter-pattered the metal roof as the factory floor was plunged into darkness.

"Is he gone?" asked the boy in the green-striped shirt.

"I don't know," replied the boy in the red overalls, looking around the room at the bins of glowing green bones that now faintly illuminated the factory.

"He is gone," said the little girl in the aqua dress with the pink ribbon. "We have precious little time to waste."

CHAPTER 3

The three little children worked through the night to clean up the factory the best that they could. No small task, given that they had never stayed up this late before, but by sunup they had done it. They groggily met the other factory children at the employee door the following morning and laid out their plan.

"Factory King is gone for good," said the little girl in the aqua dress and pink bow. "Our terrible bully is not coming back. He has left us in charge for the last day of work."

All around the factory the children smiled and clapped their little hands at the news that their tormentor would not return.

"Do your jobs as usual today and make the cheap plastic skeletons," said the boy in the red overalls. "If we finish early, we all go home early with our full wages. And then… we are free!"

The children rushed to their workbenches and laughed as they quickly assembled the last of the plastic skeletons.

They had completed their work before lunch, and as a reward, the children took any food or drinks they wished from Factory King's fridge inside the factory office. The sauce baijiu was quite popular.

Shortly after lunch, a truck showed up at the factory loading dock to pick up the assembled and packaged plastic skeletons.

"Hello, children. I am here to pick up the plastic Halloween decorations," said a businessman in broken Chinese stepping from the truck. "Please tell Factory King that Mr. Scooper is here."

"He is not here," said the boy in the green-striped shirt. "Factory King left this morning, but he told us you were coming."

"He seemed very… distraught," added the girl in the aqua dress with a slow shake of her pink-bowed head.

"I do hope Factory King does not do anything rash," said the boy in the red overalls as he turned to the children crowded around the loading dock. "Fill the truck for this man!"

"Oh, well, sure. As long as you have my Halloween orders ready for pickup, I'm good as gold," the businessman said with a polite smile. "Did he mention how he wished to be paid?"

"Factory King told us to collect the payment," said the boy in the green-striped shirt. "You can give the money to us."

"No," the little girl in the aqua dress and pink bow said as she stepped forward and held out her hand to the businessman. "He said I was to collect the payment, because I am the best at math and most trustworthy."

Neither the boy in the green-striped shirt nor the boy in the red overalls knew any math, and they nodded in agreement that the little girl was trustworthy and should receive the payment. They also now knew what she was capable of.

The businessman shrugged and handed a thick envelope stuffed with cash to the little girl, who opened it and looked inside.

"I trust that it is all here?" the little girl said, looking up at the businessman. "You are to be trusted?"

"Oh, yes," the businessman said with a chuckle and another polite smile. "It is all there. I'm a man of means. You can trust me."

"Count this," the little girl said to the little boy in red overalls, and handed him the envelope full of money, before turning back to the businessman. "Please do not take offense, Mr. Scooper, but being well off does not make you trustworthy."

"No offense taken," the businessman said, throwing up his hands. "You are a very wise young lady."

The payment was in full and the last of the boxes of plastic skeletons were loaded onto the businessman's truck. As the truck full of skeletons drove away from the loading dock, the children laughed and jumped and played. The little girl in the aqua dress divvied up the money from the envelope equally amongst the children, who cheered and celebrated as they skipped, and ran from the factory.

The little girl took Factory King's dog-shooting gun from his office and met the boys outside the factory.

"Do it," she said.

The boy in the green-striped shirt opened up a bright

red gasoline can and poured fuel all along the walls of the factory. The boy in the red overalls lit the match.

"We must never speak of this," said the little girl in the aqua dress and pink bow as they watched the High Quality Novelty Company factory go up in flames. The two little boys nodded in agreement.

All of the factory children had fled before the fire trucks arrived. Any records of the children were lost in the factory fire.

When later questioned, Mr. Scooper, the businessman who had been to the factory before the fire, remembered only that the factory owner had been quite distraught and might have done something rash. The factory was a total loss, but the inventory had already been shipped. The factory foreman was missing and presumed dead. No insurance claim was ever filed. The case was soon quietly covered up and dismissed by authorities.

...

After weeks at sea, the giant cargo ship, under the command of an American sea captain named Seaward, pulled into port on the West coast of the United States. Using gigantic cranes, the hulking ship was quickly emptied by port employees and the big metal shipping containers were stacked in tidy rows just inside the port.

"That appears to be everything," said a strapping young port employee holding up a clipboard and pen. "Who's signing for the cargo?"

"That t'would be I," said Captain Seaward, taking the clipboard and marking it with a big 'X.'

The port employee reached down to scan a tracking barcode on one of the shipping containers when a dull thud came from deep inside the container, followed by the sounds of shuffling, then another dull thud.

"Did you hear that?" asked the big port employee as he put his ear to the metal doors of the container. "It sounded like someone was pounding on the door."

The port employee opened the lock on the shipping container, threw the bolt, and slowly pulled the metal door open with a long, loud creak. The muscly port employee shrieked with fright as a plastic skeleton propped against the metal door fell forward and came to rest face down in the dust.

"'Tis but a cheap plastic skeleton," laughed the sea captain as he tapped the plastic skull of the skeleton with the toe of his thick rubber boots.

"That scared me half to death," said the port employee as he pulled himself together and regained his composure. "I nearly crapped my pants."

"Taint my problem no more, lad. Best of luck to ye," said the gnarly old sea captain as he indelicately handed the clipboard bearing his signature to the young port employee, and quickly headed back to the deck of his ship.

The port employee put the glowing plastic skeleton back into its cardboard box, resealed the metal shipping container, and supervised as the cargo was loaded onto the back of an awaiting semi-truck. The truck driver, a bald, bearded man, wearing thick black goggles, black rubber gloves, and a trucker hat, honked the horn of his big rig and laughed maniacally as he drove out of the port in a cloud of acrid black diesel smoke.

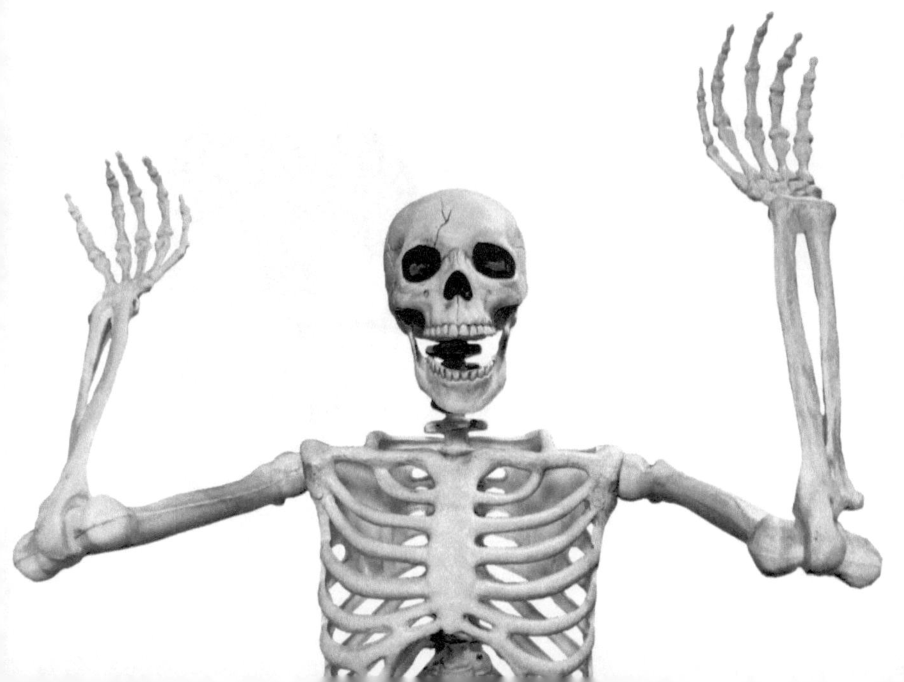

CHAPTER 4

Sean Brawner slid the razor blade out of his box cutter and ran it along the clear plastic tape seam of the cardboard box. The store's shipment of Halloween merchandise had arrived on the delivery truck that very afternoon, and he would be the first to see all of the new Halloween decorations. Sean had specially requested the assignment from the manager on duty and was grinning like a kid tearing open a birthday present.

"Yes! Score!" Sean cheered as he pulled a cheap plastic skeleton out of the box. "Let the Halloween fun begin!"

Oakley Bellend, neither a fan of Halloween nor seasonal retail planograms, set down his box cutter and looked up from a box of rubber bats and spiders to give Sean a quizzical look.

"Are you for real?" Oakley said. "It's just a dumb skeleton."

"I'm big into Halloween," Sean said as he pulled out his cell phone and opened the messaging app. "I'm helping my uncle do a huge Halloween display in his yard. And since I'm working here I can tell him when all the new stuff arrives and he can come get it first."

"That matters?" Oakley said.

"To him it does. He always tries to outdo his

neighbor," Sean explained, as he snapped photos of the three plastic skeletons folded up inside the box with his phone. "I've helped him put the decorations up every year since I was, like, in elementary school. It's a whole thing. It's even been on the news."

Sean hit send and messaged his Uncle Gerry the photo at the exact moment Assistant Store Manager Tad Dearie walked by and noticed Sean holding his phone.

"No phones on the floor, Sean," Tad scolded cheerfully.

"Sorry, Tad," Sean said. "I'm just really excited for Halloween."

"Oh, me too! My wife has a whole little ceramic Halloween town she sets up on my puzzle table," Tad said, casually leaning on a merchandise cart stacked high with boxes. "Yep, rows and rows of these little, extremely breakable, ceramic haunted houses. And every time I look at them, let me tell you, I just count the days until Halloween is here so I can get my puzzle table back."

"Fascinating," Oakley said sarcastically, his eyes practically rolling out of his head as he opened a box of plastic candy corn lights.

"Yeah, my puzzle table is perfectly positioned so I stay out of the middle of the living room with my puzzles, but I'm still able to see the TV without bending my neck too far. Because that's where I have all my problems. My neck," Tad said as he rubbed his neck.

Sean's phone buzzed. His uncle had replied, "Hoorayy I'll be right there," followed by "R the skeletons glow in the dark?!"

"Because that's why I have the puzzle table in the first place. I couldn't see, let alone hear, the TV all the way over in the dining room. Sometimes I think she knows that, ahhhhh," Tad sighed as he picked up a box of candy corn lights and began to absentmindedly place them on the corresponding shelves. "Anyway, no phones on the floor, mister."

Oakley shook his head at Sean, who kneeled in front of an open box of foam tombstones, marveling at them like a golden retriever. Oakley opened a box of sexy women's Halloween costumes.

"I just love Halloween! All the new spooky stuff," Sean said as he sliced into another box. Inside he found adorable stuffed birds made of felt wearing little felt Halloween costumes. "There's all this cute Halloween stuff for moms and little girls. Lawn decorations for the dads. It's just too fun!"

Sean regarded the box of tombstones and Halloween costumes as Oakley opened a box of grotesque masks and shoved it across the floor to him.

"You've got all the sexy Halloween costumes for sexy girls and basic Halloween costumes for guys not trying to scare the sexy out of the girls. And then, you have these," Sean said and pulled a realistic snarling werewolf mask from the box and yanked it on over his head. "Creepy as fuck masks that nobody finds attractive. The really scary ones."

"That's not scary, dude," Oakley said as he dropped his box cutter into the pocket of his employee vest.

Sean turned to silently stare at Oakley, giving him a

blank look through the eye holes in the werewolf mask. Oakley shook his head in disappointment.

"Shhh," Sean whispered as he held up a finger to the werewolf mask's snarling snout, then crept up behind the shelves where Tad was still stocking candy corn lights.

"Boo!" Sean shouted as he jumped out from around the shelves at Tad.

"OH! OH NO! HELP! POLICE! JESUS! SWEET LORD JESUS! NO! NOOOO!!!" Tad shrieked as he fell to the floor, writhing in terror and sobbing as he let out the tiniest of farts. "Don't eat me! No!!! PLEASE, I don't want to die. I don't want to die. I don't want to DIE! NOOO…oooo…ooo…oo…"

"Tad!" said Sean as he raised his hands in reassurance.

"AHHH! It knows my name!" cried Tad as he scrambled across the floor and threw cardboard packaging at Sean.

"Tad! Tad!" Sean said and ripped off the cheesy werewolf mask. "It's just me, Tad. Sean. It's just a mask."

"Oh! Oh, Sean… Sean," wheezed Tad. "I thought you were a werewolf."

"Nope," said Sean. "Just a mask."

"Like, an actual real life werewolf, right there in front of me! I really thought I was a goner there," Tad laughed nervously, getting to his feet. "Phew, am I relieved you're not a werewolf."

"Nope," said Sean, "just a Halloween mask."

"Because I was so worried I was going to have to shoot you," Tad said and pulled a pistol from the waistband of his pants as he shook his head and chuckled to himself. "I was, like, seconds from blowing your head clean off. Seconds!"

"Just a mask, Tad," said Sean, giving Oakley a nervous, side-eyed glance.

"Man, that would have been a rough night, huh? Blam!!!" Tad laughed as he pretended to shoot the pistol. "Oh, what did you do at work tonight, honey? Oh, I just shot an employee, who I thought was a werewolf, in the throat. Blood everywhere! Because what a mess that would have been."

"Mask," gulped Sean.

"Oh… you. You, you, you. OK, well, I better find a bathroom quick, because I nearly just about pooped myself a little there. Phew," Tad sighed with relief as he put the pistol back into his waistband, then shot finger guns at Sean as he walked away toward the front of the store laughing. "Nearly crapped my pants right there in the aisle. Too funny, I'm gonna get you back. You."

"I'd like to see you try," Sean laughed, returning the volley of finger gunfire as Tad walked away, before turning to Oakley. "Did you know he had a gun?"

"Yeah. He got it after last Black Friday," said Oakley as he set down the box of inflatable spider lawn decorations he had just opened and picked up another. "I wish you wouldn't do that."

"Do what?" asked Sean, perplexed.

"Get all friendly with the managers. See, it's bad enough we have to stay here late tonight setting this shit up," Oakley said as he opened a box of cheap plastic cat skeletons, "but if you make Tad like you, he's going to want to hang out and help all night."

"Other than maybe the gun, he's not that bad," Sean said. "Maybe we'd even get done a little faster."

"Right. And then neither of us can use our phones all night," Oakley said, "and that would be bad. Got it?"

"I suppose you're right," said Sean.

Sean opened a box of ghost-shaped cookie cutters and skull-shaped cake pans. Perfect for grandma, he thought.

More vibrant plastic spilled from the shipping boxes as the evening continued. There were bags of rubber monster finger puppets and novelty fake eyes for spooky grandpas, autumnal play-it-safe pumpkins covered in leaves and bags of fluffy spider webs for the religious types who equated Halloween with Satanic worship, and even Halloween-themed pet toys for pets and Halloween pet costumes for people who like having their pets hate them.

Something for everyone on the spooky spectrum. Sean felt like he had died and gone to sweet, sweet Halloween heaven. Or hell, as the case may be.

Oakley opened a plastic bag of little cheap plastic skeletons. Also packed in the same box were several cheap plastic dog and spider skeletons.

The sounds of raspy breathing and heavy footfalls in tennis shoes moved toward the Halloween section at high speed from down the main store aisle. Sean and Oakley both stopped and looked up from their boxes.

"I'm here. I'm... it's me. I'm here," gasped an

exasperated middle-aged tattooed guy, with a long, graying beard and a horror movie t-shirt, as he pushed an empty shopping cart into the Halloween aisle. "I understand you have… hold on… you have the skeletons, that… gotta catch my breath… you have the plastic skeletons that I need. Skeletons. Give… Give them to me. Please and thank you."

"Hey, Gerry," Sean said as he held up a freshly unboxed plastic skeleton for his uncle to see. "Oakley, this is my Uncle Gerry."

"Sup," wheezed Gerry as he clutched a stitch in his side and took a puff from an asthma inhaler. "Sean here is staying with me while he goes to school, so I guess you could say I'm his older, much cooler roommate."

"Hey," said Oakley, with a nonchalant nod and a flip of his hair.

"Much, much cooler roommate. The coolest," Uncle Gerry said and clapped his hands together as he got his bearings amongst the Halloween boxes. "Right, so skeletons!"

"How many do you want?" asked Sean.

"All of them. No! How much are they? Wait!" Uncle Gerry huffed. "I keep talking about this. Treat yourself, Gerry. Self-care is important. You can finally finish your skeleton pirate ship. You deserve this. I'll take three."

"Only three?" Sean said, not believing his ears.

"Three is reasonable, right? I mean, I do still need to convince Rhonda that I've always had 'em," Gerry said as he loaded three full-size plastic skeletons into his cart as quickly as possible. "Any more than three and her bullshit detector's gonna go off. Rhonda does not like how much I spend on my Halloween shit."

"She does not," confirmed Sean, turning to Oakley. "Rhonda is Gerry's girlfriend."

"Almost common law aunt now, thank you," Uncle Gerry said, beaming as he pumped his fist. "Man, I'm just super stoked to get me some more skeletons!"

"Why do you need that many skeletons anyway?" Oakley asked. "Like, how big is your Halloween display?"

"He doesn't know," Gerry said in amazement.

"He doesn't know," Sean confirmed.

"He really doesn't know?" Gerry retorted.

"What don't I know?" asked Oakley.

"He really doesn't know," said Gerry.

"What don't I know?!?" demanded Oakley.

"My uncle's Halloween display is somewhat legendary in town," Sean said. "It's a pretty big deal."

"Big damn deal! It's been on the news. Made the paper. Even got it up on that internet thing once, on the... the..." Gerry waved his hand and snapped his fingers at a loss for words.

"Tumblr," said Sean.

"On the Tumblr," Gerry said proudly. "So, you see, when one's Halloween display has reached an almost celebrity status amongst the esteemed members of one's own community, one is also sorta expected to improve upon one's Halloween display with each passing year. Oneself."

"Right," said Oakley, not seeming to understand in the slightest.

"Good plastic skeletons always sell out early and," Gerry continued, "unless you want inferior, tiny, or cartoony skeletons, you have to be ready to pick up the good ones right away when they arrive. And THAT is how you put your neighbor's Halloween display to shame."

"And a pirate ship full of skeletons does that?" Oakley asked, cutting open a new box.

"Not just skeletons. Pirate skeletons!" Uncle Gerry said. "This year Ernie Kolchich is going down."

"Mr. Kolchich is his neighbor," Sean said.

"Kolchich!" Uncle Gerry hissed. "My plastic pirate skeletons are going to blow his stupid inflatable jack-o-lanterns away!"

"OK, I think I get it," said Oakley, still not getting it. "We also got some of those inflatable decorations…"

"Inflatables are the lazy man's Halloween decoration," Uncle Gerry said. "People put them on timers, so they end up looking like deflated garbage bags during the day. Only amateurs and bozos have them. Full display, all the way, or don't play."

"Fair enough," said Oakley as he opened another box, looked down, and quickly shoved the box across the floor to Sean. "Right, well, nope. I'm not touching those."

"Oh, sweet," said Sean as he pulled a long, boney, plastic snake skeleton from the box. "Snake skeletons! Want one, Gerry?"

"Fuck, no," Uncle Gerry said, visibly shivering. "Snakes are fucking creepy. Get that thing away from me."

Sean walked over and began to hang the snake skeletons on the metal pegs in the aisle. Uncle Gerry rooted through the open Halloween boxes, gleefully plucking terrifying treasures, which he unceremoniously tossed into the cart with his plastic skeletons. Oakley opened a box of small plastic animal skeletons and pulled out a rat and a toad.

"I'll take one of those parrot skeletons," Gerry said, rubbing his hands in excitement. "That'll look great on my skeleton pirate captain's shoulder."

Oakley reached into the box, grabbed a cheap plastic parrot skeleton for Sean's uncle, then opened the last box on the stockroom cart to find a mix of plastic costume weaponry: butcher knives, meat cleavers, and plastic pirate swords.

"Is that all of it?" Gerry asked.

"Yeah," Oakley said. "For today."

"Our manager said we'd be getting more stuff in our next shipment. Maybe in a day or so," Sean said as he flattened a box and placed it on the empty metal stockroom cart. "See anything else you want?"

"No. Yes. Crap. OK, I'll take three of those pirate swords, a plastic knife. The one with the skull on the handle from that box you just opened, please and thank you," Gerry said as Oakley handed him an armload of plastic steel. "And, that's it."

"You sure?" Sean asked.

"And one of those plastic axes. That's it. I'm done," Uncle Gerry said, turning to Sean. "Rhonda gets back from her sister's tomorrow evening, and I'd appreciate some discretion about my recent plastic skeleton purchases. Capiche?"

"Sure thing," laughed Sean. "Your secret... is safe with me."

"Alright, catch you at home," Gerry said to Sean, as he wheeled his cart around and headed for the registers. "Smell ya later!"

Oakley used his foot to nudge a box of plastic cat skeletons down the aisle and began to fill a shelf, while Sean pulled out several full-sized plastic skeletons and hung them from hooks in the shelving.

"Your uncle seems pretty dope," Oakley said.

"He's a pretty laid-back dude to live with," Sean said. "And staying at his place sure beats living in a dorm or driving back and forth to my parent's house. Plus, he grows his own weed, so that's rad."

"We are gonna hafta talk," said Oakley as he neatly arranged the plastic cat skeletons in a tidy row.

Uncle Gerry, out of breath once again, wheeled his cart of decorations back into the Halloween aisle.

"Forget something?" Sean asked Gerry with a smile. "Another plastic skeleton? Maybe the gentleman would be interested in taking home a plastic crossbow or perhaps a lovely toad skeleton?"

"No, I was too excited and almost forgot," said Gerry, swirling his fingers over the cartload of Halloween decorations. "Employee discount?"

"Oh, right! Yes," Sean said, turning to Oakley. "I'll be right back. I have to go up to the registers to use my discount."

"Hurry back," Oakley said as he started another row of plastic cat skeletons on the shelves. "Tad expects us to have all this Halloween shit on the shelves before we can go home tonight. And, I do NOT want to be here any longer than I have to be."

"I'm only gonna borrow him for a minute," Gerry said, turning his cart around, and heading back toward the front of the store.

"I'll be right back. Five minutes tops," Sean said as he jogged down the aisle after his uncle's cart, leaving Oakley alone in the Halloween aisle.

"I've got this terrible feeling it's going to be a very long night. Huh, kitty?" Oakley said as he gave one of the plastic cat skeletons a little pat on the skull and returned to work.

CHAPTER 5

Sean reached up and placed a plastic skeleton on top of a cardboard display of blow mold pumpkins and Day of the Dead plastic candy skulls at the very center of the Halloween section. Oakley sulked near the back wall and stocked the last of the inflatable Grim Reapers and Frankenstein monsters. He paused momentarily to admire the shelf of inflatable display models as their fans whirred and they began to fill with air.

"That's all of it now, right?" asked Sean as he adjusted the skeleton on the cardboard display, so its spindly plastic legs hung playfully over the sides of one corner.

"We still need to get these boxes back to the crusher," Oakley said as he broke down a box with his box cutter and tossed it onto the metal cart. The store's intercom speakers crackled annoyingly in the ceiling overhead.

"Great job… <pop> Hello? <hiss> Great job today, team!" Tad's voice blasted through every speaker in the entire store. "The last customer just left, I locked up the front of the store, and we are closed for the night, people. And I've also got paychecks to hand out, so that's fun. So, yeah, come see me before you all leave and I'll give you your stubs…"

A smattering of sarcastic applause came from the various employees scattered throughout the store.

"And, here it comes," said Oakley with a roll of his eyes.

"Here what comes?" asked Sean.

"Sean and Oakley," Tad's voice boomed overhead. "You two can keep working and come see me after you get those boxes crushed. I'll have your paychecks ready for you in my office."

"Fuck," groaned Oakley, "will this night ever end?"

Sean placed the remaining flattened boxes on the cart and started to wheel it toward the stockroom but froze as something caught his attention out of the corner of his eye. He shook his head and rubbed his eyes, making sure his mind wasn't playing tricks on him. Where did that sword come from, he wondered.

"That's hilarious," Sean laughed, pointing toward the cardboard center display. "Did you put that sword in the skeleton's hand?"

"No," said Oakley, as he started to walk toward the stockroom. "Come on. Let's get this over with."

"Yes, you did," said Sean, giving the skeleton with the sword another puzzled look as he pushed the cart out of the Halloween aisle after Oakley.

"Did what?" said Oakley.

"Put that sword there," said Sean. "You had to have done it."

"No," said Oakley, "I didn't."

"Well, I know I didn't put that sword in its hand, and we were the only ones back here, so it had to be you," Sean said as he pushed the big swinging stockroom door open with the cart. "Come on, quit messing with me."

"It wasn't me. It was probably just Tad," Oakley said, following Sean into the stockroom.

"What?" Sean said. "But, Tad was in his office."

"He was probably getting his "favorite employee" back," Oakley said, making the air quotes. "Why? Are you scared now?"

"No," Sean laughed as he wheeled the metal cart of flattened and stacked cardboard up to the box crusher. Oakley loaded the cardboard into the machine, lowered the big metal safety gate covered in warning stickers cautioning to keep arms, legs, and hands out of the crusher, then hit the big red button on the wall.

The noisy crusher activated with a hydraulic hiss. The boxes crunched and crackled as they were smashed into a tight bundle at the bottom of the machine. Sean and Oakley were both transfixed as they watched as the big machine brought mechanical destruction to the cardboard.

Sean briefly looked over to the roller conveyor belt that led from the store loading dock to a sorting area further inside the stockroom. A single box of plastic skeletons had somehow been overlooked and sat alone on the conveyor belt.

"I guess we missed one," Sean said as he walked across the loading dock to the conveyor belt.

"Just open it up quick and give me the boxes so we can get the hell out of here," said Oakley as he watched the compressor inside the box crusher begin to rise. "Just dump the skeletons on the floor or something and we'll deal with them tomorrow."

Sean opened the box and found three plastic skeletons neatly folded up and grinning inside. Oakley raised the safety gate on the box crusher and loaded the rest of the cardboard from the metal cart inside. Sean pulled the plastic skeletons from the box, set them on the concrete loading dock floor, and handed Oakley the last box. Oakley chucked the box into the machine, unflattened.

"I'm hoping for an extra satisfying crunch," Oakley said.

"Me too," said Sean, as he pushed the empty metal cart to the side of the box crusher. "That's the last box."

"Let's get this done, grab our checks, and get the fuck out of here," Oakley said reaching for the box crusher's safety gate.

"Heh heh heh, ha ha ha!" came a bonetinglingly, evil cackle from behind them.

CHAPTER 6

Sean and Oakley both froze. The hair on the backs of their necks stood on end as they each held their breath and turned around toward the source of the demonic laughter.

Three cheap plastic skeletons stood upright near the conveyor rollers. The plastic skeleton in the middle wore a black cat ear headband. The two plastic skeletons that stood at its sides held box cutters. A phantasmal green glow haloed their cheap plastic bones. And, they were laughing.

"Heh heh heh, ha ha ha!" the plastic skeleton in the black cat ears cackled, then raised its arm slowly, and pointed at Sean and Oakley.

"Ahhhh! The skeletons are laughing!" screamed Sean, backing toward the box crusher. "What do we do!"

"Dude, no. Chill," Oakley said as he regained his composure. "Tad is just fucking with us."

The cheap plastic skeleton in the cat ears shook menacingly, or as menacingly as it could, being a cheap plastic skeleton in dopey cat ears. Oakley stifled a laugh, which appeared to deeply displease the plastic skeletons.

In a loud creepy voice, the plastic skeleton in the cat ears began to angrily yell something at Sean and Oakley in Chinese. The glowing plastic skeletons at its side swung their box cutters and slashed at the empty air between them.

If either Sean or Oakley knew how to speak Chinese, they would have been treated to a truly terrifying monologue by the plastic skeleton in cat ears about their paranormal origins and the true nature of their evil intentions. It went something like this:

"I am Factory King and my spirit is trapped in the very glowing bones of the cheap plastic skeletons I once produced in my factory," the cheap plastic skeleton in cat ears shouted, shaking its outstretched plastic arm. "Tonight, as the moon rises on the time somewhere between September and October when they put out the Halloween stuff, I rise from the dead to replace the bones of the living with the glowing bones of my cheap plastic skeletons from hell, so that I, Factory King, may once again walk the world of the living and usher in an era of hell on Earth. Do not resist me. You are doomed. Prepare to die, stock boys, and give your flesh suits to me! Heh heh heh, ha ha ha!"

But what Sean and Oakley heard was just a bunch of loud Chinese nonsense, which they didn't understand, coming from a cheap plastic skeleton shaking around in a stockroom. The tone was clearly angry and scary, but it was still all gibberish to them. And, of course, the cheap plastic skeleton that had shouted at them was wearing cat ears.

Oakley burst out laughing immediately. The sight was so ridiculous that even Sean began to let down his guard.

"Fuck, dude. That is so lame," Oakley snorted,

examining the plastic skeletons for strings. "Very funny, Tad! You can come out now!"

If the cheap plastic skeletons could have expressed emotions on their fleshless plastic skulls, they would have looked both angry and confused. The specter inside the plastic bones of these petrochemical poltergeists, the one calling himself Factory King, had spent the entire journey across the ocean inside the shipping container from China working on this speech. He had not expected such a nonplussed reaction.

My speech was about haunted bones and flesh suits, Factory King thought, and it should have killed. Literally and figuratively. It was really, really creepy stuff, so why are these stupid stock boys laughing?

"I'm not buying it anymore, Tad," Oakley yelled toward the back of the stockroom as he gave one of

the plastic skeletons a little shove. "Come on out. I just want to get my paycheck and go home."

"Oakley!" Sean yelled. "Watch out!"

The plastic skeleton on the far left started to walk toward Oakley as it waved its box cutter, the razor blade glinting in the low light of the empty stockroom. It did not appear to appreciate being mocked.

"Oh, they walk, too?" Oakley said sarcastically. "Very funny, Tad. Ha ha."

"Heh heh heh, ha ha ha!" laughed the plastic skeleton in the cat ears as it pointed threateningly at Oakley.

"Ha. Ha. Ha," Oakley laughed back at the skeleton as he slow-clapped.

"HEH HEH HEH, HA HA HA!!!" laughed all the skeletons at once.

"Ha. Ha. Ha," Oakley deadpanned. "Seriously. Knock it off."

The cheap plastic skeleton in cat ears shook with rage. If he had blood, it would have been boiling.

"Attack him at once!" the skeleton in the cat ears shouted in unintelligible Chinese, as it growled with frustration at Oakley.

The plastic skeleton on the left lunged forward and swung its box cutter. The blade sliced through Oakley's t-shirt, and opened a shallow three inch long gash on his chest. It came as such a surprise to Oakley that it took a moment for the cold, rising sting of the blade to reach his brain.

"Ow! Fucking fuck! That thing just fucking cut me!" Oakley yelped. "Tad! This is NOT fucking funny."

"I really don't think Tad is doing this," Sean said as he grabbed the metal stockroom cart and aimed it at the advancing plastic skeleton. Oakley jumped out of the way as the skeleton swung the box cutter at him again.

"Stop, dude! I'm fucking bleeding!" Oakley yelled and patted the bloody cut oozing beneath his shirt. "This is fucking crazy, Tad. Too far! I'm serious."

"Heh heh heh, ha ha ha!" laughed the plastic skeleton with the box cutter as it lunged again at Oakley, stabbing the box cutter threateningly in front of itself.

Sean shoved the metal cart across the stockroom. The cart slammed into the plastic skeleton, which crashed down onto the cart, before it sailed off into the darkened corner of the stockroom.

The other plastic skeleton with the box cutter roared as it rushed toward where Sean was standing and swung its box cutter in wide arches as it approached. Oakley grabbed a mop from beside the box crusher and swung for the skeleton. The strings of the mop connected with the skeleton's plastic skull with a wet slap and knocked it head-over-heels inside the box crusher cage.

"Aight. That's it," growled Oakley as he slammed the safety cage shut. "Now I'm pissed."

Oakley hit the big red button on the wall with the bottom of his fist and the box crusher began to compress. Cardboard crinkled and flimsy plastic bones popped and snapped inside the machine. The glowing plastic skeleton's bony legs stuck out from inside the crusher and began to thrash around wildly as the skeleton was twisted and smashed into the bale of compressed cardboard at the bottom of the crusher.

"Run!" yelled Sean as he bolted from the loading dock and made for the door.

"Heh heh heh, ha ha ha!" laughed the cheap plastic skeleton in the cat ears as it started to walk menacingly after them. There were no strings. There were no wires, gimmicks, or gears. The cheap plastic skeleton was walking all by itself, and it was not happy.

Sean and Oakley, running, slammed into the swinging stockroom door and fled for their lives out onto the empty store floor.

CHAPTER 7

"What the actual fuck are those?!" Oakley yelled as he and Sean bolted from the stockroom.

The cheap plastic skeleton in the cat ears laughed gravely as it reached the doorway. The big swinging door swung back fast and sent the plastic skeleton reeling backwards into the stockroom.

"I don't know what they are, but we've got to get the hell outta here!" Sean yelled as he ran through the nearest store aisle.

"I thought you were Mr. Halloween? Aren't you supposed to know about these things?" Oakley said as he stopped in his tracks just short of the Halloween section. "Dude, where are we going? Like, what's the plan here?"

"Stay alive? Run? I don't know," Sean said. "Maybe we should go find Tad?"

"To do what? Charm the pants off some living skeletons?" Oakley said. "So, we've just got to stay away from these things and get out of the store alive. That's it? Right? Easy enough."

"Um, Oakley?" Sean gulped and pointed to the Halloween aisle. Slowly, Oakley turned to look at what Sean had seen.

"Oh, shit!" he yelped in surprise.

An entire end cap display of cheap plastic rat skeletons had come to life and, one by one, began to leap from the shelves. Their little plastic rat bones glowed with the same lime green radiance as the full size skeletons. Some of the rat skeletons had lost their tails or arms as they clattered down onto the hard tile floor. And then as a swarm, the rat skeletons began to scurry across the floor toward Sean and Oakley. The broken plastic rat skeletons limped and clawed after their unbroken brethren.

"What do we do?" Sean said, his eyes wide with fear.

"Up here," Oakley said as he jumped onto the freshly filled shelves of a medium sized end cap display covered in plastic pumpkin candy bowls.

Sean climbed up onto the raised shelving right before the first plastic rat skeleton reached the display. Oakley used his foot to clear the display shelves of pumpkin bowls. Just in case, he told himself.

The plastic rat skeletons scrambled and drummed their little plastic arms fruitlessly against the metal shelves, the effect of which was that of rolling thunder. But the display shelf was too tall for the small plastic rat skeletons to jump up on, and they squeaked with rage as they scurried around on the floor and tried to find a way up the shelving.

Oakley reached over into the Halloween costume aisle and grabbed a pack of plastic ninja swords for himself and a witch's broom, which he handed to Sean.

"What's this for?" asked Sean, holding up the broom in confusion.

"For hitting," said Oakley as he tore the plastic ninja swords free from their packaging. "Hit them."

"What?!"

"The rats! Hit them!"

A few plastic rat skeletons had puzzled out that they could climb the fabric of the Halloween costumes and were beginning to scramble up capes and colorful costume bodysuits toward the top of the shelves. Sean swung the broom wildly and knocked the rat skeletons back down to the tile floor, where most shattered. But their tiny broken pieces kept moving.

Suddenly, the swarm of plastic rat skeletons quit trying to climb up the shelves and instead began to flee.

"Eek!" squeaked the plastic rat skeletons as they scampered off down the costume aisle. They were terrified… of something.

"That was close," sighed Sean, wiping the sweat from his forehead with his sleeve. "But, what would make those plastic rats run away like that?"

"Oh, fuck. Not that. Anything but that," Oakley said and squirmed against the shelving as he pointed to the glowing green cheap plastic snake skeletons that slithered up the aisle towards them. "Oh, fuck! Fuck, no! Hit those motherfuckers with your broom, dude!"

"What is happening?!" asked Sean.

"Hit them!" Oakley shrieked. "If they bite you, you get plastic poisoning or something!"

"Well, I'm not sure that's how it works, but…"

"HIT THEM, DUDE!!!"

Sean waved the witch's broom at the plastic snake skeletons as they began to creep, crawl, and climb up the end cap. Oakley clambered up higher on top of the shelves and held out his plastic ninja swords in self-defense.

Sean's broom clacked against plastic snake skulls as it made contact and sent several plastic snakes clattering across the tile floor. But unlike the rat skeletons, the snake skeletons were able to stretch, twist, and contort their boney bodies up to the top of the end cap display. And, they were much more determined.

Sean, nearly overwhelmed by the onslaught of plastic snake skeletons, climbed up to the top of the shelves behind Oakley.

"Just keep them away from me!" Oakley cried as he motioned with his ninja sword for Sean to keep the snake skeletons at bay. He turned toward the store's back wall in search of an escape route, and frankly, to avoid pissing himself at the nightmare creeping towards him from the floor.

Oakley screamed as a cheap plastic monkey skeleton leapt in front of him on the top of the shelves. The monkey skeleton hissed and waved a plastic flashlight with a pumpkin on the end at Oakley.

"Some of these skeletons aren't that scary," Oakley said, his voice still quavering. "This monkey skeleton is actually kinda cute."

Suddenly, the store lights went out, plunging the Halloween section into darkness, and a deep, maniacal laugh filled the air.

"HEH HEH HEH,
HA HA HA!"

CHAPTER 8

The plastic monkey skeleton switched on the pumpkin flashlight and shined the beam directly beneath its tiny plastic fangs, illuminating a shadow of a monkey skeleton on the back wall of the store that stretched all the way to the ceiling.

"Eeh eeh eeh, ooh ooh ooh," laughed the cheap plastic monkey skeleton. Sean and Oakley both screamed.

Loud clomping footsteps thundered toward the Halloween section. Sean and Oakley exchanged frightened looks. Even the plastic monkey skeleton seemed intrigued by this new sound.

"It was me! It was just me, you guys!" Tad shouted from several aisles over as he jogged through the store. "I just turned off the lights in the store, so you can, you know, stop with the screaming."

Tad bounced into the Halloween section wearing a leather motorcycle jacket and a round open face motorcycle helmet. He held his keys and two paycheck envelopes. Tad looked up at Sean and Oakley standing on top of the shelves, then around the Halloween decorations at all the broken plastic rat and snake skeletons, and his mouth fell open.

"Sean? Oakley?" Tad stammered. "What on Earth is going on here? Why are you two on top of the shelves?"

Then he looked to his right and arched his eyebrows in confusion. What he saw somehow explained everything and also, somehow, explained almost nothing. Tad pointed at a row of small 16-inch plastic skeletons hanging on pegs along the aisle.

"Did that little plastic skeleton just move?" Tad asked, his mouth hanging open in shock. The little plastic skeletons all turned their miniature skulls to glare at him. Tad shook his head in surprise. "They're looking at me! And, I think they're angry."

"It's the cheap plastic skeletons!" said Sean.

"From hell!" Oakley added. "They've come to life!"

Suddenly, a horde of full-sized cheap plastic skeletons dressed in Halloween costumes marched into the middle of the Halloween section, and laughed as they waved plastic swords, scythes, and nunchucks.

"HEH HEH HEH, HA HA HA!!!"

"Oh, dear lord!" Tad shrieked as the little plastic skeletons began to pull themselves off the shelf pegs, one by one. Tad bolted from the Halloween department. "Everybody run for your lives!"

The plastic monkey skeleton threw his pumpkin flashlight at Oakley, who ducked, and sent the flashlight sailing into the back of Sean's head.

"Hey, you two," Sean said. "Stop monkeying around."

"No, dude," Oakley scolded Sean. "It is absolutely not the right time for that."

The plastic monkey skeleton grabbed one of Oakley's plastic ninja swords out of his hand and threw it at Sean. Sean batted it away with his witch's broom. Oakley swung his remaining sword, hit the monkey skeleton, and launched it through the air.

The plastic monkey skeleton landed hard on the tile floor several aisles over, its cheap plastic arm snapped clean off at the shoulder. The monkey skeleton picked up its broken arm, threw it at a full sized plastic skeleton in a clown Halloween costume, then pointed up at Sean and Oakley with its remaining hand. The full-sized plastic skeletons in Halloween costumes turned to face them.

The little plastic skeletons finished pulling themselves from their pegs and assembled at the base of the shelves. From a bin, they grabbed plastic knives that were painted with fake blood and took off running through the store after Tad.

Oakley and Sean walked across the top of the shelves as the cheap plastic skeletons approached. A wave of cheap plastic spiders hopped from their shelf and began to crawl up the fabric Halloween costumes hanging in the aisle to the top of the shelves. Oakley looked around, saw the coast was clear, then leapt from the top of the shelving unit and into the center of a big inflatable pumpkin on the back wall.

Sean swung the witch's broom and swatted away the growing throng of glowing plastic spider skeletons. Plastic skeleton hands clutched and reached for Sean's pant legs, as the full-size skeletons began to climb the shelves themselves.

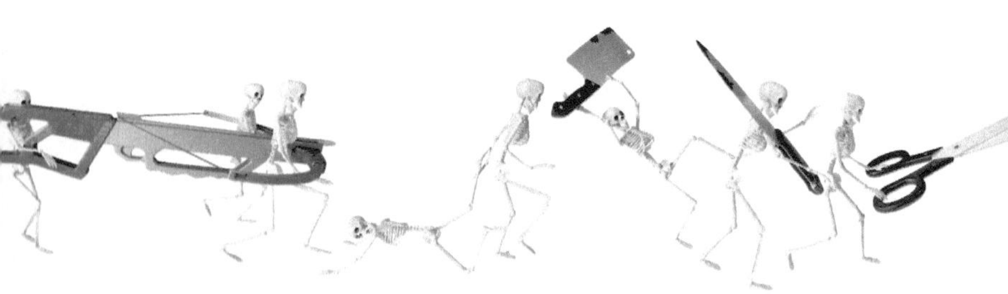

"Jump!" Oakley yelled to Sean as he turned and bolted from the Halloween section, a group of spider skeletons clacking across the tile floor after him.

Sean jumped off the top of the shelves just as a plastic skeleton dressed like an Egyptian pharaoh reached the top shelf. An inflatable Grim Reaper on the back wall broke Sean's fall. He tumbled into the aisle, dropping the witch's broom, as the cheap plastic skeletons rounded the corner and shambled towards him, swinging their plastic weapons and laughing.

"Heh heh heh, ha ha ha!"

CHAPTER 9

Tad jammed the paycheck envelopes and his keys into his leather jacket pocket and ran shrieking into the kitchen gadget aisle. The mob of small skeletons followed closely behind, each armed with a plastic knife.

"Oh my god! Stay away from me!" Tad shrieked. "I have to warn you that I am armed, and I am not afraid to shoot you!"

"Heh heh heh, ha ha ha!" laughed the little skeletons in unison.

"Ahhh!" Tad screamed in fright. "Somebody! Anybody! Help!"

A display of very sharp, very real knives in the kitchen aisle stopped the little plastic skeletons in their

tracks. The skeletons looked down at their fake plastic Halloween knives and then up at the rack of razor sharp cutlery. They tossed away their plastic knives and began to scale the shelves toward the real McCoy.

The little plastic skeletons yanked and pulled the knife display pegs down off the wall and dropped the packages of knives down to the shelves below. The little skeletons on the ground tore open the packages, brandished their new blades, and took off sprinting after Tad.

"No! No! No! I just wanted to go home tonight, do a puzzle, and watch the news!" Tad screamed as he ran as fast as he could through the office supply aisle. "What is going on?! Why are these little skeletons chasing me?! Help! No!!!"

...

Sean fell backwards over a beanbag chair laying in the middle of the floor in the home decor department. He scrambled to his feet in a panic and backed quickly away. The cheap plastic skeletons in Halloween costumes clattered and clicked and glowed, nearer and nearer, waving their plastic pitchforks and machetes and clubs.

"Yeeeee-ha ha ha!" laughed a plastic skeleton dressed like a cowboy.

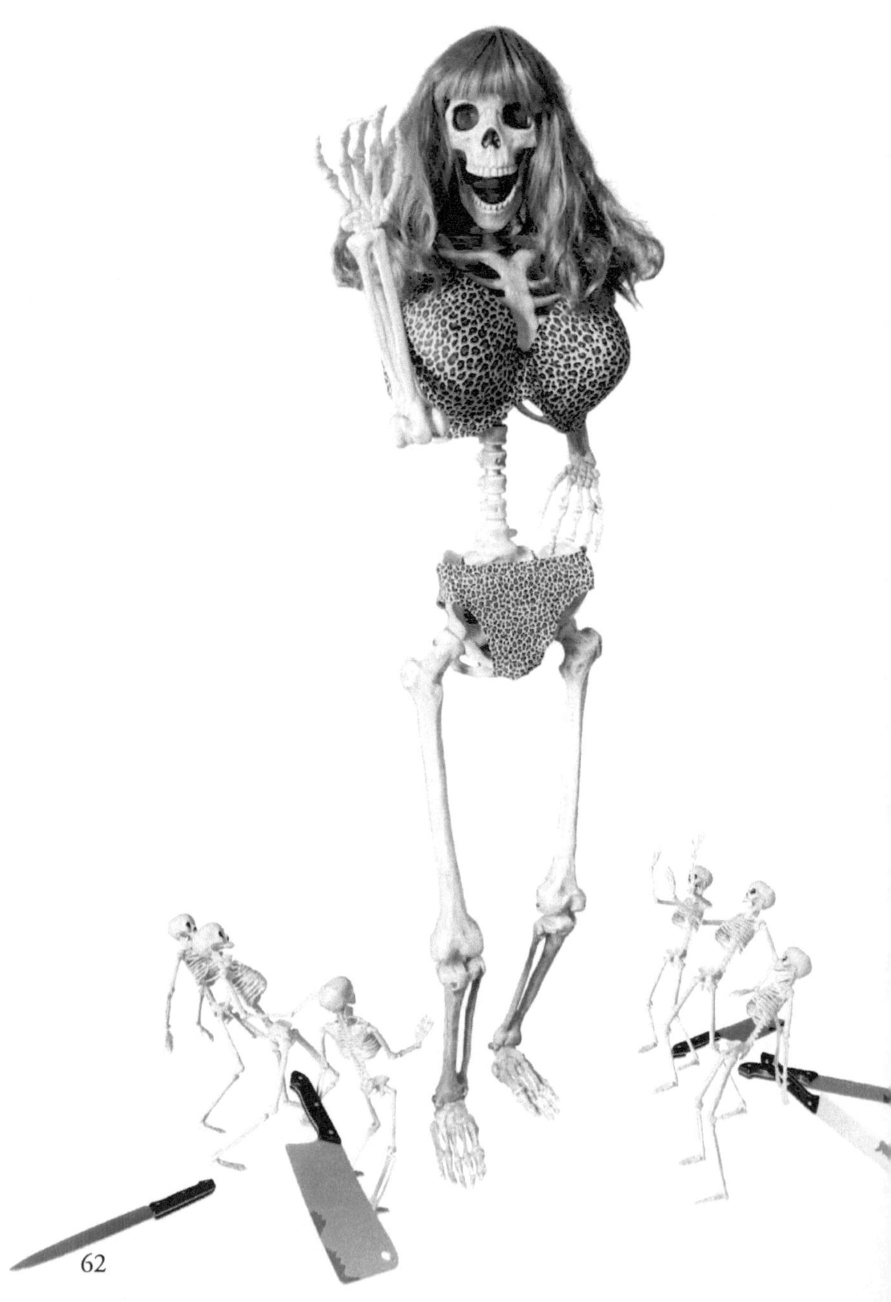

"Stay away from me!" Sean screamed.

Sean's eyes darted around the home goods, and he had an idea. He reached for the end caps and shelves, throwing anything he could grab into the aisle to slow, or perhaps even stop, the cheap plastic skeletons. He tossed clothes hampers, which the skeletons kicked away. He lobbed a vacuum cleaner, which proved to be a bit more of an obstacle. He also threw a bunch of, um, throw pillows into their path, but the plastic skeletons just clumsily climbed over them, and kept moving.

"What stops these things?" Sean wondered aloud as he pushed a shelf full of decorative baskets into the aisle behind him.

"Heh heh heh, ha ha ha!" laughed the skeletons at the very minor inconvenience.

...

Tad had just rounded the corner near the women's clothing department with the little plastic skeletons still hot on his tail. His eyes were drawn to a cheap plastic skeleton dressed in a matching bra and panty set that stood amongst the racks of the lingerie section.

"Sweet spookbinding spiders!" Tad gasped.

The sexy lingerie plastic skeleton blew Tad a kiss, and he screamed in terror as he continued his frantic run through the store, pursued by the parade of murderous mini skeletons.

. . .

Oakley used his ninja sword to swat at the cheap plastic spiders that stalked him as he ran past an aisle of coffeemakers and into the cleaning supply section of the store. Up ahead, he could see Tad dodge a stack of carts in the store's main aisle as a gaggle of little plastic skeletons chased him.

Oakley stomped on a plastic spider, when out of nowhere, a cheap plastic skeleton in a kung fu costume cartwheeled into the main aisle and waved a plastic butterfly sword at him.

A plastic skeleton in a horned barbarian helmet loudly bashed a display of adhesive bandages behind Oakley as another plastic skeleton in a ninja headband did a forward flip into the main aisle and swung a foam nunchuck in Oakley's direction.

"Heh heh heh, ha ha ha!" cackled the plastic skeletons in unison as they advanced.

"Do you boneheads want to fight me?" screamed Oakley, swinging his plastic ninja sword as he kicked the last plastic spider skeleton halfway across the store. "Fight me!"

"Haaaaa!" the plastic skeleton in the kung fu costume yelled as it stepped forward and swished its plastic sword through the air in a figure eight.

"Ahhhhh!" Oakley yelled, raising his sword to block the skeleton's attack.

Oakley and the kung fu skeleton clashed, their plastic swords thwapping hollowly against each other as they battled. But Oakley gained the upper hand, knocking the sword from the kung fu skeleton's hand, as he kicked the skeleton backwards across the main aisle and into an aisle of vacuum food sealers and slow cookers. The victory was short-lived as the plastic skeleton with the ninja headband swung its nunchucks in a blur of plastic as it advanced.

"Heads up, asshole!" Oakley yelled and struck the ninja skeleton in the neck with his plastic ninja sword.

The ninja skeleton's skull separated from its torso and flew into a cleaning supply aisle. Oakley gave a loud cry of rage and tore open his employee vest.

"Heh heh heh, ha ha ha," laughed the cheap plastic barbarian skeleton stomping toward Oakley from the soap aisle, waving its big plastic battle hammer over its head. The plastic skeleton in the kung fu costume had also just regained its footing. Behind it, sprang a cheap plastic cat skeleton that hissed at Oakley.

The barbarian skeleton swung the plastic battle hammer. Oakley ducked and the hammer crashed into a shelf of foaming hand wash refills. The plastic cat skeleton yowled as the liquid soap splashed and spread in a puddle across the tile floor.

The kung fu skeleton slipped in the slick soap suds and crashed down onto the tile, followed immediately by the barbarian skeleton, which brought down another shelf of liquid soap with its hammer as it fell.

Oakley turned and made for the front doors. The soapy kung fu skeleton tried to throw its plastic sword after Oakley, missed by a mile, and sent the sword clattering hollowly across the floor.

The plastic skull of the decapitated ninja skeleton rolled out from the cleaning supply aisle, followed closely by the plastic cat skeleton, which grew disinterested, and chased playfully down the aisle after Oakley.

"Hiss hiss hiss, purr purr purr!" meowed the plastic cat skeleton.

The headless ninja skeleton torso crawled out of the cleaning supply aisle frantically searching the floor for its missing skull.

"No! Nooo! NOOOO!" Tad screamed from somewhere near the front doors as a gunshot rang out.

CHAPTER 10

"Nooo! Stay back!" screamed Tad as he fired another shot from his pistol at the little skeletons. With his other hand, he scrambled to locate the keys inside his leather motorcycle jacket that unlocked the closed automatic doors at the front of the store. "You can have my wallet. Take my jacket. My bike! Maybe you want my bike?! I'll open the electronics stockroom and you can take everything. How about I open the store safe for you? Please! You can have anything you want, just please don't kill me! Please."

The little plastic skeletons ran toward the door and held their glistening metal knives menacingly aloft.

"Heh heh heh, ha ha ha!" the little plastic skeletons laughed.

Tad found the keys in his pocket, fumbled at the automatic door lock, then dropped his keys on the floor.

"Fudge!" Tad cursed as he reached to pick up his key ring and fired more bullets at the little plastic skeletons as they closed in on him.

One of the little skeletons was struck in the hip and the bullet sent tiny plastic bone fragments sailing into the cart corral. Tad finally found the right key and stuck it in the keyhole. He wasn't even able to turn the key in the lock before the little plastic skeletons reached his legs and began their gruesome attack.

"It feels like tiny knives are stabbing into my legs!" screamed Tad as his legs began to buckle underneath him. "Ahhh!!! Tiny knives ARE stabbing into my legs!"

The little plastic skeletons stabbed, and poked, and slashed at Tad's calves and ankles with their blades as he screamed and tried to remain standing. The pain was excruciating and as Tad fell to his knees in a pool of his own blood, he desperately grabbed at the locked automatic door, and tried to kick the little plastic skeletons away with his feet.

"Ouch! Oh my god! Stop it, you!" Tad screamed. "Somebody help me, please! I'm being stabbed to death by little plastic skeletons! And it hurts! A lot!"

The little plastic skeletons climbed all over him, and stabbed, and stabbed, and stabbed him until he was covered in tiny oozing cuts from all the stabbing. Then they stabbed him some more. You've likely heard of "death by a thousand cuts"? Well, this was like that, only with little plastic skeletons armed with steak knives. It was most unpleasant.

Blood sprayed up onto the automatic door glass. Tad screamed his last, fired one more fruitless shot, then threw his gun at the little skeletons in desperation.

Tad slumped backwards and his motorcycle helmet clonked hard against the glass. Groaning, he smooshed himself as close as he could against the automatic door. His hands left bloody streaks on the glass as he made his final stand. Soon, the little plastic skeletons had overwhelmed him.

...

Sean ran down the main aisle from the electronics section while the army of full-size plastic skeletons in Halloween costumes chased after him. Even for as fast as Sean could run, it seemed as if the cheap plastic skeletons were gaining on him.

"Heh heh heh, ha ha ha!" the cheap plastic skeletons laughed.

Sean reached the children's clothing section. He grabbed a rack of little boys' jackets and tipped it over into the store aisle. He did the same with a rack of boys' pajamas. The plastic skeletons were slowed, but not deterred, and they cackled and laughed with glee as they climbed over the fallen racks with ease.

A cheap plastic skeleton in a black werewolf mask leapt over the racks, knocked over a plastic skeleton in a wizard costume, and landed gracefully on its feet on the other side of the clothes racks, closely followed by a pack of barking cheap plastic dog skeletons.

"Heh heh heh, ha-WOOOOO!" howled the werewolf plastic skeleton.

Sean's blood flowed like ice in his veins. He looked back and screamed, as the plastic skeleton in the werewolf mask and the plastic dog skeletons bounded in his direction. Sean pushed a small kiosk of houseplants in front of them as he ran backwards down the aisle. The werewolf plastic skeleton let out a low growl in anger.

Sean nearly lost his footing as he overturned a rack of dresses from the girls' department into the aisle and stumbled past the greeting cards toward the front of the store. The surprisingly nimble werewolf skeleton jumped the overturned houseplant kiosk, and the baying pack of plastic dog skeletons simply ran around it. Sean neared the front aisles of the store as the werewolf skeleton, with the loud dog skeletons barking close at its heels, leapt over the clothing rack.

Sean made it to the registers and screamed as he turned around to see the werewolf skeleton leap into the air, ready to pounce, and much, much closer than he had expected.

Suddenly, the screech of rusty shopping cart wheels pierced the air. Oakley ran down the front aisle toward the registers pushing a stack of carts, which he rammed into the side of the werewolf skeleton with enough force to send it flying across the carpeted floor of the clothing department.

The platoon of costumed skeletons howled with rage as they continued their march through the aisle. The plastic dog skeletons growled as they reached Sean and Oakley. The plastic cat skeleton that had playfully bounced down the aisle after Oakley, stopped in its tracks, hissed as it saw the pack of baying skeletons pooches, before turning tail and running away.

The plastic dog skeletons sniffed the air with their noseless skulls, growled hungrily at the plastic cat skeleton, and then gave chase to the skeletal cat through the store as they barked their bony little heads off.

"You sure saved my ass," Sean said to Oakley.

"Don't mention it," Oakley said as he guided the stack of carts toward the front door. "Help me push these around the corner. We're going to have to bust our way through the doors."

The carts drifted across the tile as they made their turn. Sean grabbed the cart handle and gave a hard shove. With both Oakley and Sean pushing, the line of carts gained speed rapidly as they aimed the makeshift battering ram at the closed automatic glass door.

The throng of full-sized skeletons in Halloween costumes ran right behind them, laughing as they waved and stabbed the air with plastic scimitars, magic staffs, crossbows, wrenches, bones, maces, and all manner of other plastic weapons.

Sean looked to the left of the automatic doors to where the little plastic skeletons danced with glee while stabbing Tad's lifeless corpse with their kitchen knives. Sean's stomach did a somersault and he cringed at the absolute hamburger the skeletons had made of Tad's legs and stomach.

"I think I'm going to barf," gagged Sean.

"Die already, you cheap plastic bastards!" yelled Oakley at the little skeletons as he braced his shoulder against the cart handle and prepared for impact. "Ramming speed!"

The plastic skeletons in Halloween costumes laughed, growled, and roared with sadistic delight as they cornered their quarry at the locked entrance of the store.

"Heh heh heh, ha ha ha!"

The little plastic skeletons looked up, splattered red and sticky with blood, abandoned Tad's mutilated remains, and brandished their bloody knives at Sean and Oakley, as the carts barreled towards the big glass entrance.

CHAPTER 11

The carts smashed through the door in an explosion of glass. The automatic door frames were knocked free from their guide rails. Broken glass rained down on Sean and Oakley, who both shielded their faces with their sleeves as they crashed into the cool night air. Tad's corpse glistened with fresh blood and glass shards in the warm glow of the parking lot lights.

The stack of carts continued to roll forward into the empty parking lot as Sean and Oakley made a run for it. Ghostly glowing plastic skeletons in Halloween costumes poured from the store in hot pursuit.

"Now what do we do?" Sean said, his mind racing.

"We get in our cars and get the fuck out of here," replied Oakley, already pulling out his car keys. He pointed the key fob toward the employee area at the back of the parking lot and hit the unlock button on the car remote.

Little plastic skeletons clutching knives sprinted across the parking lot from the shattered store door and headed straight toward the flashing lights of Oakley's unlocked car. Sean looked over his shoulder at the undeterred plastic skeletons in Halloween costumes as he ran past Tad's motorcycle toward the employee parking area. But as Sean pulled out his own car keys, the store's giant delivery truck roared around the side of the store, fishtailed in the parking lot, and came to a stop at the edge of the parking lot facing Sean and Oakley.

"Heh heh heh, ha ha ha," cackled the plastic skeleton with cat ears, now worn over a trucker hat, from behind the wheel of the massive idling truck.

Plastic skeletons in costumes dashed through the parking lot after the two remaining store employees. Oakley made it to his car first. He had parked facing out of the space. He jumped behind the wheel and slammed the car door with only seconds to spare before the little plastic skeletons reached his vehicle.

Sean leapt into his own car and slammed the door behind him. He had parked front first and faced the street.

The plastic skeleton in the werewolf mask howled as it lunged onto the trunk of Sean's car, climbing over the roof, and bounced onto the hood. Sean screamed in terror as he pressed the button that locked his car's doors.

"Heh heh heh, ha ha ha," laughed the little plastic skeletons as they stabbed the shit out of Oakley's car tires with their knives, popping them one by one.

"Those were brand new tires, you boney bastards!" Oakley yelled through the car window at the little skeletons as he hit the ignition, threw his car into drive, and grabbed the wheel with both hands.

"Heh. Heh. Heh," laughed the plastic skeleton in the black cat ears, as it floored the accelerator pedal in the semi-truck. The big rig's tires burned rubber as they squealed on the parking lot pavement, and black smoke billowed in a great plume from the truck's exhaust. "Ha. Ha. Ha."

Sean put on his seat belt, checked his mirrors, and started his car while the werewolf skeleton pounded on his windshield.

Oakley hit the gas and accelerated. His car's shredded tires flapped and flopped around inside the wheel wells as the car began to loudly roll forward. Oakley cringed as his bare rims spun against the blacktop and sent sparks flying out behind him as his car crept through the parking lot.

"You're ruining my car's fucking finish! Fucking skeletons! Fuck!!!" Oakley yelled at the little skeletons as he pounded the car horn and his car crept through the parking lot. "My dad is going to murder me!"

More plastic skeletons in costumes encircled Sean's car and pulled at the car's locked door handles. The werewolf skeleton yanked at the wiper blades, while the rest of the skeletons hit Sean's car with their plastic Halloween accessories.

"Come on! Move, damn it!" Oakley screamed at his struggling car as he smacked the steering wheel repeatedly in frustration as a blinding bright light fixed on his car and a giant engine rumbled toward him at top speed.

Oakley turned his head and saw the plastic skeleton in cat ears laughing as it blasted the speeding semi-truck's big horn and bore down on his car. Oakley screamed in terror as the semi-truck broadsided his car, and sent sparks flying everywhere as the huge truck pushed Oakley's now destroyed vehicle sideways through the parking lot.

"Heh heh heh, ha ha ha!" laughed the skeleton in cat ears from behind the wheel of the truck.

Sean screamed as flaming chunks of Oakley's car crashed down around the parking lot. Plastic skeletons in costumes cheered as they began to climb on top of Sean's car and tear at the detailing.

"I've got to get out of here!" said Sean to himself as he threw the car into reverse and checked his mirrors again as he slowly backed over a plastic skeleton dressed like an archaeologist.

"Sorry," said Sean as the archeologist skeleton

crunched beneath his car tires. The costumed skeletons howled with rage as they pounded Sean's car with their plastic weapons.

Sean put his car in drive, hit the gas, and sped away across the parking lot in the opposite direction of the semi-truck. Costumed skeletons began to fall from the roof of Sean's car and clatter to the ground as he accelerated.

A mob of angry little cheap plastic skeletons ran in front of Sean's car and waved their knives, but Sean sped right over them, crushing their little glowing bones into bits on the asphalt. Sean swerved the wheel side to side and sent more plastic skeletons teetering from the car's roof as his tires squealed, and he fled the store parking lot in a blind panic.

CHAPTER 12

The plastic skeleton in the werewolf mask growled as it clung to the windshield wipers with one hand while beating on the windshield with the other hand. The werewolf skeleton's spindly legs flailed around wildly as it tried to kick the hood of Sean's car. Sean snuck a peek in the rear view mirror and watched as the delivery truck wheeled around in the store parking lot and began to follow him.

Sean flipped a lever beside the steering wheel and turned on the windshield washer fluid. The plastic skeleton in the werewolf mask yelped and recoiled from the wiper fluid spray. As the werewolf skeleton let go of the wiper blades, it slowly began to slide off the hood of the car. The werewolf skeleton's boney fingers and toes screeched against the glossy finish of Sean's car as it scrambled fruitlessly to keep itself from falling. Its howl was a crescendo as it slid off the hood, and under Sean's car. The werewolf skeleton's ribcage exploded into shards of plastic as it went beneath the wheels.

The speeding semi-truck crashed through the tidy big box store landscaping, drove over the sidewalk, and knocked down a fire hydrant, showering the truck in a blast of water.

"Heh heh heh, ha ha ha!" laughed the plastic skeleton

in the cat ears from behind the wheel of the semi as it careened into the street and began to pick up speed.

Unlike the plastic skeleton in the semi, Sean had the advantage of actually knowing where he was going. He took a hard left at the hardware store. He could see the poor employees through the store windows as they were brutally attacked by plastic skeletons that had armed themselves with shovels, power tools, and chainsaws. Strips of torn flesh flew through the air inside the store, and blood fountained against the store windows and painted a lawnmower display bright crimson. Sean looked away to avoid getting sick, but the smell of fresh blood hung in the air.

"Heh heh heh, ha ha ha!" laughed the plastic skeleton in the black cat ears as it took the semi through a wide, screeching left turn onto the street after Sean's car.

"Oh shit!" Sean yelled, snapping out of his daze as he floored it.

The semi-truck rumbled on not far behind, but Sean's car gained speed and opened the distance between the two vehicles. Sean weaved back and forth across the empty road in an effort to fake out the skeleton as the semi-truck belched thick black smoke behind him.

A ride-share car sped up the road in the opposite direction and swerved dangerously as it neared Sean's car. The driver screamed and flailed around in the driver's seat as two plastic skeletons, one dressed as a football player and the other as a cheerleader, boxed his ears from the backseat with their skeletal fists. Sean watched in the rearview mirror as the car went out of control and crashed into a coffee hut on the side of the road.

The big rig's horn blared in celebration behind Sean as it ejected another plume of exhaust and gained more ground. The plastic skeleton in the driver's seat snickered with delight as large chunks of the coffee hut flew through the air.

Sean hurtled down the road toward a big intersection. The road was empty and the light was green, but Sean could hear a siren approaching. Sean slowed down and carefully looked both ways. And it was a good thing he did. With blaring sirens and spinning emergency lights, a fire truck driven by a plastic skeleton in a firefighter's uniform skidded through the intersection as it took a sharp turn directly in front of Sean and barely missed clipping his car. A whole squadron of plastic skeletons dressed as firefighters clung to the sides of the big, red fire engine.

Slamming on his brakes had cost Sean major ground, and the cat-eared skeleton in the big rig bore down on him. But, Sean knew this neighborhood and had an idea.

Sean stomped on the gas pedal. The semi-truck was now almost close enough to nudge Sean's bumper. But Sean swung his car wide into the oncoming lane, still at considerable speed, and made an unexpected sharp right turn onto a residential side street. The plastic skeleton in the cab of the truck had not anticipated this.

"Heh heh heh, ha ha huh?" said the plastic skeleton in cat ears as it tried and failed to make the turn. The skeleton jackknifed the large semi, crashed the truck into a bus stop shelter, and sent sparks, glass, and twisted metal flying into the road.

Sean kept a very close eye on his mirrors as he raced down several more residential streets towards his uncle's house. He turned on the car radio, heard static, and hit the seek button to find a news station.

"Our top headline tonight… Cheap plastic skeletons have come to life and are attacking the city," crackled the radio. "I'm Newsman Wes Chestleydale. Tonight, police are advising citizens to avoid approaching any plastic skeletons, especially those that have come to life and gone on a murderous rampage. At a police press conference just a short time ago, we learned that these plastic skeletons are made from cheap plastic and imported from China…"

Sean slowed down as an elderly man in a bathrobe and an old woman in curlers ran out into the middle of the road. A plastic skeleton in a banana costume hurried along behind them swinging a plastic Halloween knife and axe. Sean swerved to miss the couple but squashed the plastic skeleton in the banana costume under the wheels of his car.

Sean slowed the car to a crawl and rolled down his window.

"Thank you, young fella!" wheezed the old man as he hugged his wife on the curb. "You saved us from that… that… that bananer!"

"That was a plastic skeleton in a banana costume," Sean explained out the window. "The plastic skeletons are coming alive!"

"Plastic ske… ske… skeletons?" stammered the old woman, scratching her curlers.

"Just avoid any plastic skeletons in Halloween costumes and you should be fine," said Sean as he cruised down the street.

"But what about bananers?" the old man called after Sean.

"What?" said Sean.

"Are bananers still safe?" asked the old man.

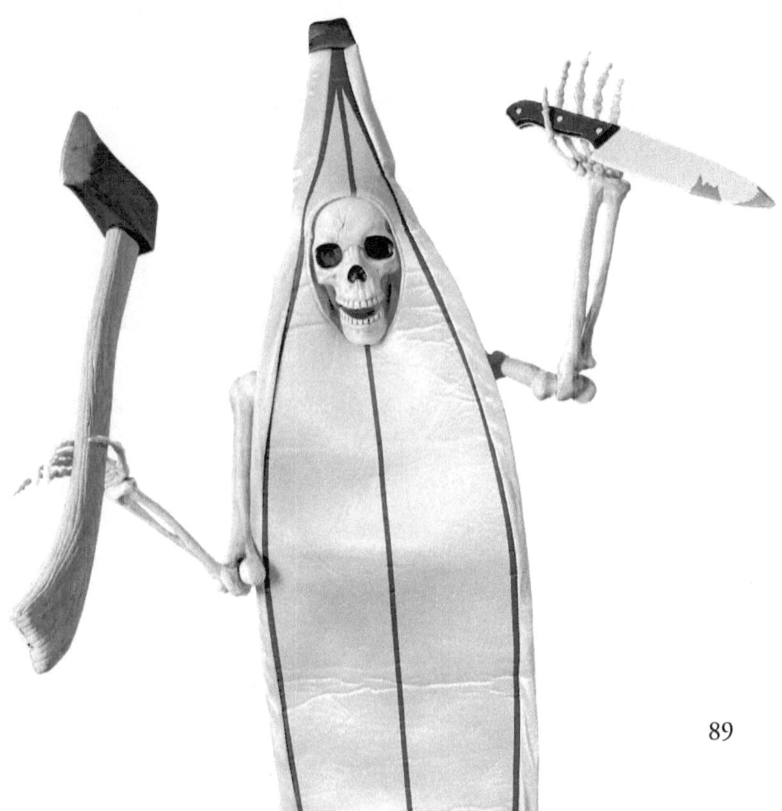

"We have bananas at home," the old woman said. "Tell him we have bananas at home."

"We have bananers at home," the old man shouted at Sean. "Do we need to get rid of them?"

"No, it's just the skeletons you have to watch out for," Sean shouted out the window as he slowly began to drive away. "Bananas are still a healthy snack and an excellent source of potassium, which is very important for people your age, especially if you have a history of high blood pressure."

"What?" yelled the old man.

"Get to safety, you two," yelled Sean. "Avoid the plastic skeletons!"

"We will!" shouted the old man clutching his robe as he and the old woman waved farewell to Sean.

"What did he say about the bananas?" the old woman asked the old man.

"What?" said the old man.

"Bananas!" screamed the old woman.

"Something about high blood pressure and safety," huffed the old man. "Kids these days. Always banging on about nutrition and safety. Pfft!"

"…police recommend staying indoors and under no circumstances should you personally attempt to face the plastic skeletons unarmed," crackled the reporter on the radio.

Sean checked his mirrors again and still didn't see the semi-truck. He eased his car down the road, a little under the speed limit, and swerved to avoid hitting a plastic cat skeleton that was being chased through the neighborhood by a barking pack of plastic dog skeletons, as well as one miniature Doberman Pinscher named Little Mister Potato Butt.

"…if you have living plastic skeletons in your home, you are advised to lock yourself in an interior room of your house and immediately call the police," the radio droned as Sean swung his car in a wide U-turn and parked in front of his uncle's house.

Uncle Gerry's house was already well on its way to being decorated for Halloween. Synthetic spider webs were draped over shrubbery, cheesecloth ghosts were hung in the bushes, and a handmade plywood pirate ship was taking shape in the middle of the front lawn.

Uncle Gerry's neighbor, Ernie Kolchich, had just parked in front of his house and was pulling a big cardboard box from the flatbed of his work truck.

"Hey there, Sean," Mr. Kolchich said as he set down the enormous box in the street and stretched out his back. "How are you doing tonight? You guys must already be getting ready for Halloween, huh?"

"Have you seen my Uncle Gerry, Mr. Kolchich?" Sean asked as he jumped out of his car and ran toward Uncle Gerry's house.

"He was doing Halloween decorating earlier," Mr. Kolchich said, pointing to Gerry's witch-that-looks-like-it-ran-into-a-tree decoration tied around the large sycamore tree in the boulevard. "That's why I was asking if you're all getting ready for Halloween. Actually, I just went to the store myself and did a little Halloween shopping…"

"Gerry! Gerry! The plastic skeletons!" Sean yelled as he pounded on the front door of the house and tried to remember which key opened the lock. "Come on, Gerry! Open up!"

"Is everything OK, Sean?" asked Mr. Kolchich with concern as he stepped cautiously away from his truck and onto the sidewalk.

"The skeletons!" Sean yelled, his hands shaking as he found the key and tried to put it into the lock. "The plastic skeletons are coming alive and attacking everyone!"

Mr. Kolchich's gaze turned to something further up the street and he slowly began to back away down the sidewalk, a look of panic on his face.

"The plastic skeletons are coming to life and they're attacking people!" Sean shouted. "Uncle Gerry!"

Sean finally got his key into the lock and heard something moving inside the house, a sound coming from just on the other side of the door. Sean held his breath as the doorknob turned slowly in his hand and the door to the house flew open.

CHAPTER 13

"It's for personal use! I was holding it for a friend! Show me your warrant!" Uncle Gerry joked as he swung the door wide for Sean. "Hey, what's goin' on, bud?"

"The skeletons are coming alive and attacking everyone!" Sean shouted as his heart nearly pounded clear out of his chest. "One chased me all the way home in a semi. This is for real."

"What? Hey, hang on for just a sec, man," Uncle Gerry said, as he poked his head out of the front door and yelled. "That's right, Kolchich, go! Get on out of here! Worry about decorating your own yard!"

Gerry walked back to the couch where Rhonda's cat was fast asleep, and grabbed his bong. Out on the sidewalk, Mr. Kolchich looked terrified and started to run as plastic skeletons in Halloween costumes chased after him down the street. Sean, out of breath and shaking, ducked inside the house and slammed the door behind him.

"Wait. Back up. So, what's going on now?" Gerry said as he took another hit from the bong and set it down on the coffee table.

"Is the back door locked?" Sean demanded as he picked up the TV remote beside Uncle Gerry's bong, changed to a local station showing news, and handed the remote to Gerry.

"OK, then," Gerry said as he gave an annoyed look to Sean. "I guess I totally wasn't watching that movie. Dick."

"Is the back door locked, Gerry?!" screamed Sean.

"Hey. Chill. Yeah. Yeah, it's locked," Gerry said, giving Rhonda's cat a pet, as he looked up at the news story on TV and his mouth fell wide open. "What's this?"

"…and police are advising people to stay indoors," Newsman Wes Chestleydale said on the television. "A note of warning for our more sensitive viewers on the videos coming into our newsroom this evening, you may find the following footage of plastic skeleton attacks… disturbing."

Images of plastic skeletons in Halloween costumes attacking people with plastic weapons began to flash across the screen. Gerry covered his mouth in shock as he watched shaky cellphone video of three skeletons dressed like fast food workers ransacking a burger joint and throwing french fries out the drive-thru window at a soccer mom in a minivan. Sean cautiously looked out the front window of the house and yanked the curtains closed.

"Is this for real?" Gerry said and pointed at the TV.

"That's what I said. Very real," Sean whispered, as he peeked between the curtains. "The plastic skeletons just attacked the store. What do we do now?"

"Don't worry, kid," Gerry said. "I've been preparing for this my whole life."

"Really?" said Sean as he snuck another glimpse through the curtains.

"Fuck no," Gerry said. "The guy on TV said to stay away from plastic skeletons, so maybe we should just, you know, stay away from plastic skeletons."

"Right," said Sean.

"So, is this, like, affecting ALL of the plastic skeletons?" asked Gerry.

"Why?" asked Sean, as he slowly turned to face his uncle.

"No reason," said Gerry.

"Heh heh heh, har har harrrr!" laughed three cheap plastic skeletons dressed like pirates that appeared in the dining room doorway and waved their plastic pirate swords menacingly.

"Heh heh heh, SQUAWK, ha ha ha WOO-HOO!" squawked the cheap plastic parrot perched on the plastic skeleton captain's shoulder. The boney bird flapped its featherless wings and bobbed its little plastic bird skull up and down in excitement. Rhonda's cat hissed at the skeletons and quickly darted from the room.

"Ahhhhh!!!" screamed Gerry. The TV remote dropped to the floor as his fingers turned to quaking jelly. "They're REALLY alive and they're in the house!"

Gerry jumped off the couch and over the coffee table as the three plastic pirate skeletons stormed into the living room. The pirate skeleton captain stepped forward and smashed a bookcase full of knick-knacks with its plastic sword.

"My collectibles!" Gerry howled. "Seriously? What gives, asshole?"

"Heh heh heh, har har har," laughed the skeleton pirate captain.

"Fuck you, dude!" Gerry said to the skeleton as he grabbed a fireplace poker and held it out like a sword. "En garde!"

The pirate skeleton captain whacked Gerry in the head with its plastic sword.

"Ouch, jerk!" Gerry yelled and held his hand to his head as he angrily batted away the pirate skeleton's plastic sword with his fire poker.

The other two pirate skeletons lurched toward Sean, who picked up the bong and his uncle's bag of homegrown weed.

"Bad time to get high, Sean," Gerry cautioned. "And careful not to get bong water on the carpet or Rhonda's gonna kill me."

"I won't," said Sean as he set the bong and baggie of weed on the mantle above the fireplace.

"Well, what the hell are you doing then?" Gerry asked, swinging the fire poker at the pirate skeleton captain.

"This," said Sean, as he squatted down and flipped the coffee table at the two advancing pirate skeletons. The coffee table tumbled into the pirate skeletons' legs and knocked them backwards. They fell to the carpeted floor and dropped their swords before being pinned beneath the table.

Gerry kicked wildly at the pirate skeleton captain and sent it wobbling off-balance. The pirate skeleton captain lashed out and struck Gerry's fingers with its plastic pirate sword.

"Heh heh heh, har har har!" laughed the pirate skeleton captain.

"Ow!" Gerry said, switching the fireplace poker in his hands, before putting his finger in his mouth and shaking out his hand. "Fucking be careful!"

Gerry swung the fireplace poker wide with his left hand and dinged the plastic parrot skeleton on the pirate skeleton captain's shoulder. The parrot skeleton sailed across the room and careened into Gerry's destroyed collectibles bookcase. Sean ran at the pirate skeleton captain with a folding chair from Rhonda's home office setup. The skeleton captain's jaw dropped in surprise as Sean swung the folding chair and blasted the plastic pirate across the room.

"And that's how you fuckin' do that!" Sean bellowed while attempting to flex.

"Nice," said Gerry.

"Heh heh heh, har har har," laughed the pirate skeleton captain as it shook its skull and quickly got to its feet.

Sean and Gerry screamed as they jumped on top of the coffee table and crushed the other two pirate skeletons' hips underneath. Then they ran through the dining room, into the kitchen, and toward the back door. Sean reached for the door handle, but his uncle yanked him back.

"Holy shit," Gerry said in shock as he pointed down at the cat flap in the door. "Look out, Sean!"

"Fuck!" Sean yelped as he leapt back from the doorway.

Glowing plastic skeleton arms were reaching through the cat flap from outside and they clawed and grabbed viciously at his ankles.

"Heh heh heh, ha ha ha," the plastic skeletons in the backyard bellowed with laughter as they tried to get inside the house.

Sean panicked and stomped on one of the plastic arms, cracking its skeletal hand clear off. The plastic skeleton hand got up on the tips of its bony fingers and skittered around the kitchen floor between Sean's and Gerry's feet.

"The garage!" Uncle Gerry shouted and ran for the other door on the far side of the kitchen. Sean kicked the skeleton hand across the room, followed his uncle through the door to the garage, and slammed it behind him.

"Open the car!" Sean yelled as he pulled on the door handle of Uncle Gerry's SUV.

"Did YOU bring my keys?" Uncle Gerry asked sarcastically.

"Why would I have your car keys?" screamed Sean. "Oh."

"First, calm down," Gerry said. "Second, it's an SUV, not a car..."

"Gerry!" yelled Sean. "Focus!"

"OK, new plan," Gerry said and grabbed a baseball bat from the garage floor. "Grab something to hit them with. I push the garage door button and we run like hell."

Sean grabbed Gerry's electric guitar and yanked the braided cable that snaked out to the amp.

"Not my guitar!" yelped Uncle Gerry. "Come on, man."

"Gerry!" growled Sean.

"Fine. Are you ready to do this?" Gerry asked as he hit the button on the garage door. "OK. One... two... three... four... five... fucking go faster, stupid fucking garage door... seven... eight... niiiiiiiine... and GO!!!"

Sean held the electric guitar by the neck like a battle axe as he ducked under the rising garage door. Gerry cautiously jogged from the garage and looked in all directions as he waved his bat.

Mr. Kolchich ran the other way down the street pursued by a mob of plastic skeletons in Halloween costumes. Otherwise, they saw no other signs of plastic skeletons in the vicinity.

"Alright, now how about we run to YOUR car," Gerry said. "Did you bring YOUR car keys, Sean?"

Sean checked his pockets and took a deep breath in frustration.

"I don't have my keys," Sean said and rubbed his temples.

"Oooh, hurts doesn't it," Gerry mugged. "So, are your keys still in the front door?"

"Yes," Sean said, staring at the sky as he shook his head. "They're still in the front door."

"OK, well then, Einstein, new plan," Gerry said as he patted the baseball bat in the palm of his hand. "We run around to the front yard, do a MacGyver roll, you snag the keys while I watch your back, then we drive to the nearest dispensary for some edibles and get the hell out of Dodge until this whole thing blows over or Rhonda kills me. Ready?"

Sean nodded.

"Go!" yelled Uncle Gerry as he moved like a secret agent and swung his bat from side to side. "Evasive maneuvers! Side to side, Sean! Zigzag pattern!"

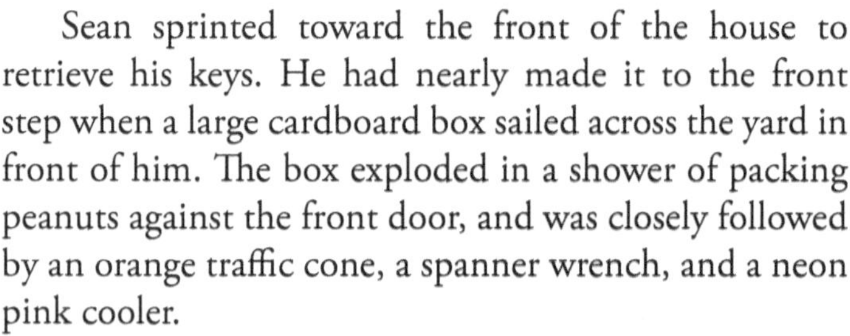

Sean sprinted toward the front of the house to retrieve his keys. He had nearly made it to the front step when a large cardboard box sailed across the yard in front of him. The box exploded in a shower of packing peanuts against the front door, and was closely followed by an orange traffic cone, a spanner wrench, and a neon pink cooler.

Sean and Uncle Gerry turned to see a plastic skeleton in a devil costume holding a monkey wrench and a little plastic skeleton with an armload of assorted spanners that it had pilfered from the bed of Ernie Kolchich's work truck. But what really troubled Sean and Gerry was the giant, glowing, 12-foot-tall, cheap plastic skeleton that effortlessly climbed out of the back of the truck.

"I can't believe it. That asshole got a giant fucking skeleton?" gasped Gerry, shaking his head. "Damn you, Kolchich! Damn you!"

"HEH HEH HEH, HA HA HA!!!" roared the giant plastic skeleton as it loomed over the front yard and headed straight for them.

CHAPTER 14

Sean and Gerry screamed in shock at the enormous scale of Mr. Kolchich's giant plastic skeleton as it slowly lumbered across the yard, stopping briefly to kick over Gerry's plywood pirate ship display, before getting ensnared in a cheesecloth ghost hanging from a string tied to a tree branch.

The skeleton in the devil costume threw the monkey wrench, which went long, banged off the hood of Gerry's SUV, and cracked his windshield.

"My car!" yelled Gerry.

"SUV," corrected Sean.

"My SUV!" sobbed Gerry, shouldering his baseball bat. "I'll kill you, you sonofabitch!"

Gerry took a step toward the devil skeleton, bat raised and ready to strike, when the little plastic skeleton lobbed a spanner that struck Gerry hard in the kneecap.

"Ow!!!" screamed Gerry, clutching his knee and hopping on one foot. "Motherfucker!!!"

The giant skeleton finally had freed itself from the cheesecloth ghost and turned to face Gerry.

"Gerry, leave it!" shouted Sean. "Run!"

They bolted out of the yard as fast as they could and ran away from the house. The giant plastic skeleton lumbered after them, flanked by the plastic skeleton in the devil costume and the little plastic skeleton with its spanners. Gerry stumbled and let out a yelp of pain as he limped along behind Sean.

"Fucking knee!" Gerry grumbled as he fell further behind, before adding. "Tell Rhonda I went running."

"What did you say?" Sean asked, breathing hard as he ran down the street.

"It's nothing," Gerry said as he winced in pain. "My knee is fucked up pretty bad."

Sean jogged back and helped steady his uncle as he desperately tried to run away. Gerry was giving it his all, but his limp had seriously slowed them down as the giant plastic skeleton clomped nearer and nearer.

"Come on! We have to get to safety," said Sean.

The giant cheap plastic skeleton blithely wandered into the front yard of a neighboring house and snatched a vintage plastic blow mold ghost from their front steps.

"Go on," Gerry said to Sean, his face contorting into a grimace from the agony he felt in his knee. "I've lived a good life. Run, Sean! Go on without me."

"What!?" Sean yelled. "Are you crazy? You can't give up at the beginning of the chase. Keep going!"

The giant plastic skeleton threw the blow mold ghost, which sailed through the air, and clonked down in the middle of the road in front of Gerry, tripping him up. Gerry hopped along on his good leg to avoid using his bad knee, which only served to slow him down even further.

"I'm not going to make it, Sean," Uncle Gerry wheezed as he clutched his knee, a look of dread on his face as he gazed back at the skeletons that chased them. "Remember me fondly."

"Just shut the fuck up and keep going!" yelled Sean as he looked around the area and tried to find a safe place for them to hide.

At that moment, a pizza delivery guy pulled up to the curb in a beat up old car that smelled faintly of weed, music blaring, oblivious to the oncoming danger.

"Sup," the delivery guy said with a nod of his chin as he stepped out of his car.

"Sup," Gerry said, wincing as he hopped down the road.

The giant plastic skeleton uprooted a realtor's 'for sale' sign from another neighbor's front yard and swung it like a club as it gained ground on Sean and Gerry.

The clueless pizza delivery guy reached into his car and grabbed his pizza delivery bag.

"Giant skeleton…" huffed Gerry to the pizza guy between hops. "Attacking… Run…"

"Huh?" the pizza guy said as he turned to look at Gerry.

"Run!" advised Sean, bearing the weight of his uncle on his shoulder. "Giant skeleton!"

"What the hell are YOU guys smoking?" said the pizza guy. Then he saw it. Then he screamed. "Ahhhhhhhh!!! Dude!!! Giant skeleton!!!"

"That's…" wheezed Gerry. "That's what I was sayin'."

The giant plastic skeleton swung the 'for sale' sign at the pizza guy and hit the roof of his car. The pizza guy dived back into the driver's seat and slammed the car door as the devil skeleton pounded on the driver's side window. The giant plastic skeleton swung the realtor sign once more, smashing the plastic pizza company light off the top of the car and cracking the car's windshield.

"Somebody help!" yelled the pizza guy, then he screamed as the little plastic skeleton popped up behind him from the back seat with an armful of wrenches.

"Maybe that'll keep... the big guy busy..." Uncle Gerry groaned between hops. "I've got... to sit down... pretty soon. Shit."

"Just keep fucking moving!" yelled Sean.

"Language..." said Uncle Gerry. "Fuck..."

Sean and Gerry gained more ground while the giant plastic skeleton was preoccupied pounding the pizza guy's car into scrap metal, and the little plastic skeleton pelted the pizza guy with wrenches.

Sean scanned the street for cheap plastic skeletons as Gerry continued to hop along, but they were both now slowed down considerably. Sean ran, dragging his uncle, until he saw bright lights radiating from the nearby park. Then he had an idea. Not a great idea, mind you, but an idea all the same.

"Into the park! The ball field!" Sean said and pointed to the fenced-in grass turf of the well-lit baseball diamond.

Behind them, the pizza guy continued to scream over his car stereo as the giant plastic skeleton shattered the back window of his car with the realty sign. Sean and Gerry reached the ball field and opened the rusty metal gate to the outfield.

The gruesome screeches of the gate's hinges sent shivers up their spines. Gerry hobbled inside the chain-link fence. Sean quickly closed the gate behind them with another loud screech and made sure the latch was secure around the metal post that held up the fence.

But the creaky sandlot gate caught the attention of the giant plastic skeleton.

The giant plastic skeleton dragged the battered 'for sale' sign on the ground behind itself, leaving a long gash in the boulevard as it tromped toward the ball field.

"HEH HEH HEH, HA HA HA!!!" the giant plastic skeleton's bones quaked as it roared with laughter.

"Heh heh heh, ha ha ha!" laughed the freshly forming mob of cheap plastic skeletons in Halloween costumes that began to flood down the deserted streets and sidewalks surrounding the park, waving their plastic weapons.

The plastic skeletons coalesced in the street behind the giant plastic skeleton as it lurched after Sean and Gerry. A strong wind surged through the trees and the sky directly over the park, and, only above the park, roiled with dark storm clouds as the skeletons all clomped toward the ball field together, booming with laughter.

"HEH HEH HEH, HA HA HA!!!"

CHAPTER 15

Sean swung the electric guitar by the neck with both hands as he gave a quick look around the vacant ballpark. He noticed the bikes, bats and balls, and jackets that had been hastily discarded on the bleachers. It was as if a late night neighborhood game had suddenly ended and been abandoned in progress.

"Where is everybody?" asked Sean as he gazed up from the ballfield to the strange green lightning that pierced through the ominous clouds swirling in the sky over the empty park. Fat raindrops pattered the ground and tinged against the metal fence posts. "Rain delay?"

"Sssss… ahhh… fuck. I really need to sit down, bud," Uncle Gerry said as he limped slowly across the outfield, using his baseball bat as a makeshift cane. "I'm definitely too old to be doing this shit. And cool. I'm too old and too cool to be doing this shit."

The giant plastic skeleton roared as it led the plastic skeleton army into the park. Sean turned and saw the giant plastic skeleton throw the 'for sale' sign overhanded like an axe toward Gerry. Sean ran back to his injured uncle and watched as the realtor sign soared through the air in what felt like slow motion but wasn't slow motion, because it was regular motion. Gerry, however, had slowed down considerably, but he had managed to limp into the clear just as the sign crashed down beside second base. The sign pinwheeled through the infield and kicked up a big cloud of sand and clay dust that was quickly swept away by the gusts of wind and rain that pummeled the park.

"Gerry, come on!" Sean yelled. "They're right behind us!"

Thunder boomed overhead just as the giant plastic skeleton reached the ballpark fence. It grinned, because how could it not, and then stepped over the fence effortlessly. But the regular sized plastic skeletons in Halloween costumes, who were much more regular sized, struggled to climb the chain link fence, and they struck it with their plastic weapons to no avail.

Swarms of plastic rat, snake, and spider skeletons climbed the metal fence and dropped with muffled thuds onto the wet grass of the outfield. The little plastic skeletons dropped their knives and climbed over the chain-linked fence. A one-armed plastic monkey skeleton threw its pumpkin flashlight over the fence and climbed over behind the little plastic skeletons.

Slowly, the costumed skeletons ambled toward the rusty ball field gate, which they again began to hit with their plastic weapons, also to no avail. But try they did.

"Get to the dugout or batting cages or whatever. That fenced-in box thing," shouted Gerry, a picture of defiance in the face of certain defeat, as he limped across the stormy infield with his bat.

Sean turned back to help Gerry and saw the giant plastic skeleton stomping through the outfield.

"Gerry!" Sean shouted as the driving rain soaked his hair and face.

"Get to the damn dugout, Sean!" Gerry yelled, as he turned to face the giant plastic skeleton. "Hey, Paul Boneyan! I've got a bone to pick with you!"

Sean hesitated, but he ran. The doorless entrance to the dugout from the field was wide open. The only gate that led to outside the dugout fence had been locked shut with a chain and padlock. Sean ran into the dugout and carelessly tossed the electric guitar in the corner, where it twanged musically in the mud. He looked around for something to barricade himself inside the dugout. With considerable effort, he strained to pick up a heavy wooden dugout bench and place it over the opening from the field.

"Heh heh heh, ha ha ha!" the plastic skeletons laughed in triumph as they finally figured out the fence latch, opened the gate in the outfield, and began to pour into the ballpark in a whirlwind of flying newspapers, plastic bags, and cardboard nacho trays. Gerry held his baseball bat high with both hands and thrashed the air threateningly as the giant plastic skeleton descended upon him, silhouetted against the sky by a blinding flash of green lightning

"You are not to scale!" Gerry screamed as he swung the bat and made slight contact with the giant plastic skeleton's hip.

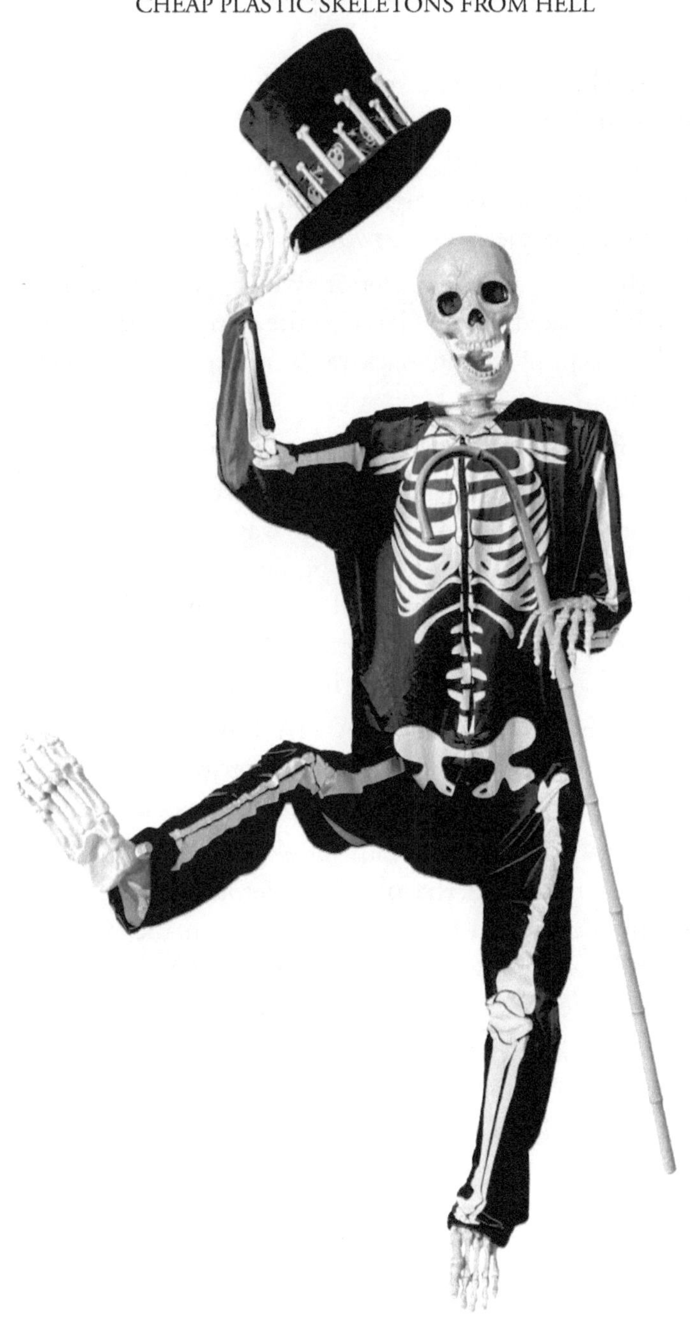

The blow opened a small split in the glue that held the plastic seam of the giant plastic skeleton's hip bone together and sent a spiraling mist of glowing green energy into the crisp night air. But, the giant skeleton stayed in one piece and now it was mad.

The giant plastic skeleton swung its massive arm, which knocked Uncle Gerry to the rain soaked ground and sent him rolling backwards toward the pitcher's mound.

"Gerry!" Sean screamed. "Get up, Gerry!"

Plastic skeletons in Halloween costumes shambled over second base and made their way onto the infield, as an endless parade of bony bodies bounded through the creaky gate. The giant skeleton turned its enormous head to glare at Sean, who grabbed another bench and leaned it against the opening in the dugout fence.

"HEH HEH HEH, HA HA HA!!!" laughed the giant plastic skeleton as it stalked angrily toward Sean, who was cornered in the dugout like a rat in a cage.

Gerry sat upright and shook the dirt and rain from his beard. As the plastic skeletons in Halloween costumes swarmed and encircled him on the pitcher's mound, Gerry swung the bat and clubbed the first plastic skeletons to try to approach him on the mound.

"Heh heh heh, ha ha ha!" cackled the plastic skeletons in Halloween costumes over the thunder, as they stabbed the air around Gerry with their plastic weapons.

"Gerry!" Sean screamed and watched in horror,

helpless, as the plastic skeletons surrounded his injured uncle.

The giant plastic skeleton arrived at the open dugout door, took a knee, and swatted the benches barricading the doorway aside. Sean screamed as the giant skeleton stuck its oversized arm deep into the dugout and began to reach for him.

CHAPTER 16

Sean's clothes were heavy with rain, and he was exhausted. He grabbed the neck of the battered electric guitar as the giant plastic skeleton's glowing plastic fingers snatched at the open air inside the dugout.

"Heh heh heh, ha ha ha!" the giant plastic skeleton roared.

"Not today, big bones!" Sean yelled as he swung the electric guitar high over his head and down in a long arch.

The giant skeleton took a direct hit to the elbow. Its fused plastic forearm separated from its body and clattered to the dugout's dirt floor in a swirl of glowing green vapors that crackled electrically in the cold autumn winds. The giant skeleton howled with frustration as its broken arm continued to claw and reach for Sean in the back of the cage.

A big group of plastic skeletons in Halloween costumes turned and lumbered through the driving rain toward the dugout opening. Sean inched backwards until his shoulders pressed into the chain link fencing of the locked dugout gate. He reached through the gap in the fence and fumbled with the chain in desperation.

"Shit!" Sean yelled, confirming the chain was held securely by a sturdy padlock. He was trapped like a skunk under a doublewide.

Uncle Gerry groaned as he used the baseball bat to stand upright on the muddy pitcher's mound.

Surrounded by laughing plastic skeletons, Gerry spun in a circle and swung the bat wildly.

"You know, you guys are really getting under my skin!" Gerry yelled and cracked a plastic skeleton in a vampire cape across the skull. "You skeletons think you're so tough… but I can see right through you!"

The horde of costumed skeletons marching toward Sean cackled as they climbed the overturned wooden benches and poured into the dugout. The space quickly became too constricted to swing the electric guitar, so Sean held it by the neck and rammed the guitar forward into the mob of attacking skeletons.

"What's it gonna take to kill you boneheads!" yelled Sean.

Sean jammed the guitar hard into the skeleton mob. He smashed the arm off a plastic skeleton in a sexy nurse costume and shoved it to the ground. He brought the guitar down hard on a skeleton in an astronaut helmet and caught a skeleton dressed like a pizza delivery guy carrying a fresh pizza on the upswing.

"Aaaahhhhh!!!" Sean screamed as bolts of jagged green lightning danced in the sky.

And while the wild winds whipped and torrential rain thrashed him, the unstoppable plastic skeletons only laughed at the futility of it all. Sean took a desperate stab at a plastic skeleton in a punk mohawk wig, toppling it in front of the skeleton mob, which simply climbed over it, laughing as they shook their plastic weapons, and pushed closer and closer to Sean.

"Holy fuck! Help! Somebody help us!" Sean shrieked

through the chain link dugout fence as the growing wave of costumed plastic skeletons continued to crush forward and overpower him. "HELP!"

"Heh heh heh, ha ha ha!" laughed the plastic skeletons as they drew nearer, their evil plastic bones clacking and clicking.

Uncle Gerry twisted around, shielded his eyes from the rain, and clubbed every plastic skull within reach. But just as soon as he had dispatched with one plastic skeleton in fairy wings, another plastic skeleton in a hockey mask would pop up to replace it.

"Don't tell Rhonda I bought more plastic skeletons!" Gerry yelled as the skeleton army overwhelmed him. He screamed and screamed, while the cheap plastic skeletons laughed and laughed.

"Heh heh heh, ha ha ha!!!"

CHAPTER 17

"Heh heh heh, ha ha ha! heh heh heh," laughed the cheap plastic skeletons, "ha ha ha! Heh heh heh, ha ha ha!"

"Gerry?" said Sean.

"Yeah, bud?" Gerry replied.

"How are you doing over there?" asked Sean.

"My knee still hurts, I'm drenched, and I'm covered in plastic skeletons, but otherwise I'm doing pretty good. You?" Gerry asked as he looked around at the plastic skeletons that weakly clattered their plastic arms and weapons against him.

Sean looked down at his own arm where a plastic skeleton in a chicken costume chewed limply at his wrist. The rains still fell and the winds still blew and the green lightning still lightninged, but outside of that, the skeletons weren't posing much of a threat.

"I'm doing fine," Sean said matter-of-factly as he shoved the dog pile of wimpy plastic skeletons away with the battered and broken electric guitar. "I think… I think unless they're armed, like with a real weapon, these things really aren't that strong."

"Yeah, I kinda noticed that myself," said Gerry.

"One was biting me, but it didn't hurt," Sean said as he climbed over the heap of plastic skeletons that had smushed into the dugout; their brittle plastic bones crunching beneath his shoes.

"Great! Good news! But one of these skeletons keeps punching me in the nuts, and it's definitely starting to hurt," Gerry said as he used the baseball bat to bash the plastic skeleton dressed like Robin Hood that was hitting him in the crotch. "Still could use a little help over here though, bud."

"Is it just me or did the rain just get a little lighter?" asked Sean as he climbed out of the open dugout door and smashed a whole row of lurching, costumed plastic skeletons to the ground with the electric guitar. The clouds above rumbled angrily, but the rain and wind began to die down. "See?"

"I think you just might be onto something there," Gerry said as he got to his feet and swung his baseball bat back and forth like a machete until he had cleared an open path toward Sean. The green lightning still flashed from deep within the clouds above, but the driving rain had diminished considerably to more of a light rain.

Scores of broken plastic skeletons now lay on the dirt of the ball field, where they snarled and groaned with frustration as Sean and Gerry stomped and snapped their plastic bones underfoot. The rain was now a mere sprinkle and the winds had died down to a stiff breeze.

"Wow, that was super crazy," Gerry said as he pulverized a plastic spider skeleton with the top of his bat. "And, I see you completely fucked up my guitar."

"Sorry," Sean said.

"Don't worry about it," said Uncle Gerry. "I'll just take it out of your deposit."

"What?!" exclaimed Sean.

"Nothing. Nothing," said Gerry as he hobbled across the field. "That deposit's already long gone anyway."

A little plastic skeleton with a knife ran across the field toward Gerry. Sean lined up his shot, swung the electric guitar like a golf club, and hit the little plastic skeleton out of the park.

"You've got to watch out for the little ones," Sean said. "They have knives."

"Got it," Gerry said as he raised his baseball bat high above his head like a caveman and clubbed another little plastic skeleton with a knife into the ball field turf. "Fuck you, little skeleton!"

Faint green lightning illuminated the dark clouds above and thunder rumbled. From the dugout, the one-armed giant plastic skeleton roared and ran at full speed toward them, as the crushed and broken plastic skeletons in Halloween costumes moaned and struggled to get to their boney feet.

"Hold on a sec," Sean said as he jumped up, swung the electric guitar wide, and knocked the giant plastic skeleton's head off. The giant skull bellowed in defeat as it bounced off toward third base. Above, the dark clouds began to roll away.

"I did not find that very humerus!" Gerry said as he bashed the giant skeleton body in its remaining arm and spun the gargantuan skeleton around. The rains had all but stopped.

Gerry swung again and knocked the legs out from beneath the giant skeleton, and sent it crashing to the ground, where it landed on top of a pile of costumed skeletons struggling to get to their feet.

"Did you hear what I did there? Sean?" Uncle Gerry asked.

"Huh?" Said Sean. "Sorry?"

"I said "I did not find that very humerus" when I hit it in the arm," Gerry said, laughing to himself.

"I don't get it," said Sean as he stomped on a plastic rat skeleton that squeaked as it cracked into pieces under his shoe.

"Like the arm bone," Gerry said, limping over to Sean and leaning on his shoulder for support. "Humorous. Humerus. Spelling's different, sounds the same."

"Homonym," said Sean as he bashed a wriggling plastic snake skeleton's skull to bits with the electric guitar.

"No," said Gerry, messing up Sean's hair. "You're a homonym, Sean. You're a homonym."

"I suppose we should go home and deal with your plastic pirate skeletons now," said Sean as he helped his uncle limp out of the park. The moon was now visible through the clouds.

"Damn it," said Gerry.

"What?!" Sean said. He tensed up and looked around the park.

"I'm gonna have to tell Rhonda I bought more plastic skeletons now," said Gerry, "and she's gonna kill me."

CHAPTER 18

"The cheap plastic skeletons were initially thought to be a major threat to the community," Newsman Wes Chestleydale said on television, "but were later found to be mostly harmless, once disassembled."

"And that's the last of 'em," Uncle Gerry said as he handed Sean a wiggling plastic garbage bag full of destroyed pirate props and plastic skeleton bones. "Time to take out the trash."

"Nice," said Sean as he exhaled a thick cloud of weed smoke across the living room and set down the bong on the dinged up coffee table.

"Did that sound cool?" Uncle Gerry asked, plopping down on the couch, picking up the bong, and giving Rhonda's cat a quick scratch behind the ears.

"What? Take out the trash? Kinda," Sean said as he headed for the door with the writhing trash bag of bones. "How's your knee?"

"Been better, been worse," Gerry said, patting his knee brace as he sparked up and cashed the bong. "Battle damage, dude."

"…police are recommending double bagging the disassembled animated plastic skeletons inside two drawstring trash bags before placing them in the recycling bin for pickup," blared the TV. "I'm Newsman

Wes Chestleydale. We'll have more on this story, as well as our continuing coverage of a serial killer on the rampage. Is he still in our area and is your family in danger? Find out during our noontime news update."

"That's about enough of that," Gerry said as he switched the TV to a horror movie marathon and packed another bowl.

The air was crisp outside, but the sun had risen high enough to burn off the dew. Sean looked around at the destruction on the street as he went to the curb and dumped the wriggling bag of plastic into the recycling bin. Ernie Kolchich stepped out onto his front porch. He also held a wiggling garbage bag of his own and had a big bandage over a large fresh cut on his forehead.

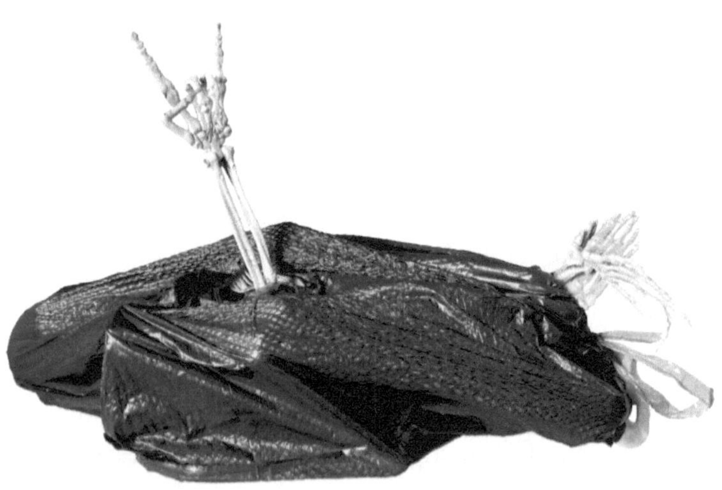

"Hey, Sean," Mr. Kolchich said. "Survived the night, huh?"

"That we did, Mr. Kolchich," Sean said, "that we did."

A recycling truck turned the corner and rumbled down the street. The green recycling bin by the curb rocked side to side in protest.

"How's your uncle?" Mr. Kolchich asked.

"He's…" Sean started to say.

"Get on out of here, Kolchich! Git!" Uncle Gerry yelled from the porch. "Keep your eyes on your own Halloween display! Ya hear me? I'll know if you copy me, asshole!"

"Gerry's the same as ever," said Sean. "Sorry, but we had to smash your giant plastic skeleton last night."

"I figured as much," said Mr. Kolchich as he deposited the garbage bag of thrashing plastic skeleton bones in his own recycling bin. "No worries. I've still got a hologram projection ghost that'll knock your socks off, so I guess I'm not quite done with Halloween yet."

"Gerry's also got a few more tricks up his sleeve, too," Sean said as he headed back toward the house. "Sorry. I need to go down to the police station and give a statement about last night. I better get a move on."

"I won't keep you," Mr. Kolchich said as he shut the lid of his recycle bin and waved goodbye to Sean. "Tell Rhonda hello for me when she gets back."

The recycling truck driver used the truck's big mechanical arm to lift Uncle Gerry's shuddering recycling bin and dump it into the back of the truck.

Bags and bags of wiggling plastic skeletons groaned and yelled "No!" inside the recycling truck as it crushed and compacted its load.

"Kolchich has a hologram ghost," Sean said as he walked around Uncle Gerry and back into the house.

"Son of a bitch! Really? A hologram ghost? How am I going to top that?" Uncle Gerry said under his breath, before yelling next door. "I'm watching you, Kolchich!"

☹ EPILOGUE

At the municipal recycling center, plastic bones rained down from gunky conveyor belts and into large bins, where they tumbled and tossed along with soda bottles, milk jugs, and lunch meat tubs. The discarded plastic refuse rolled off another conveyer belt to be sanitized and sorted. And yet another conveyor whisked the clean plastic away to be dumped into a massive plastics crusher, where they were smashed and smushed tightly together into large rectangular bundles, ready for reuse.

A large semi-truck pulled into the recycling center parking lot and began to reverse into the loading dock with a beep, beep, beep.

A bald man with a long beard and dark black goggles stepped out of the passenger seat of the big rig wearing a gray coverall jumpsuit and thick black rubber gloves. He smiled broadly, revealing two rows of rotten yellow teeth, like a crocodile with major periodontal problems.

"Hello," said the man in the goggles. "I'm a Recycled Plastic Acquisitions Specialist."

Recycling center employees began to lift bale after bale of recycled plastic into the back of the man's semi-truck using a forklift, then shoved each bale neatly into place with good ol' fashioned elbow grease.

The bald bearded man in the jumpsuit stood in a sunbeam, his eyebrows dancing suspiciously as he grinned his rancid grin and watched the truck being loaded up with plastic. The recycling center employees later reported nothing particularly usual about the man, except for two details: One, that the man's left arm shook and twitched uncontrollably the entire time he waited, and two, that he smelled very strongly of cilantro. Make of that what you will.

The last of the plastic bales were finally loaded onto the semi-truck trailer. A recycling center employee rolled down and latched the truck trailer door, banged on the side of the truck, and waved goodbye. The bald bearded man in the jumpsuit and goggles flashed his sickening smile one more time, and waved farewell out the window of the truck, which spewed a great big cloud of dark diesel fumes into the air as it rumbled away down the road.

Just out of view of the recycling center employees, the cheap plastic skeleton in black cat ears sat behind the wheel of the semi-truck. Between the plastic skeleton and the bald bearded stranger sat the bloody, perforated corpse of Tad Dearie, still wearing his motorcycle helmet and leather jacket.

"Drive!" the man in the dark goggles said to the cheap plastic skeleton in cat ears with a sinister giggle.

"Heh heh heh, ha ha ha!!!" the cheap plastic skeleton laughed.

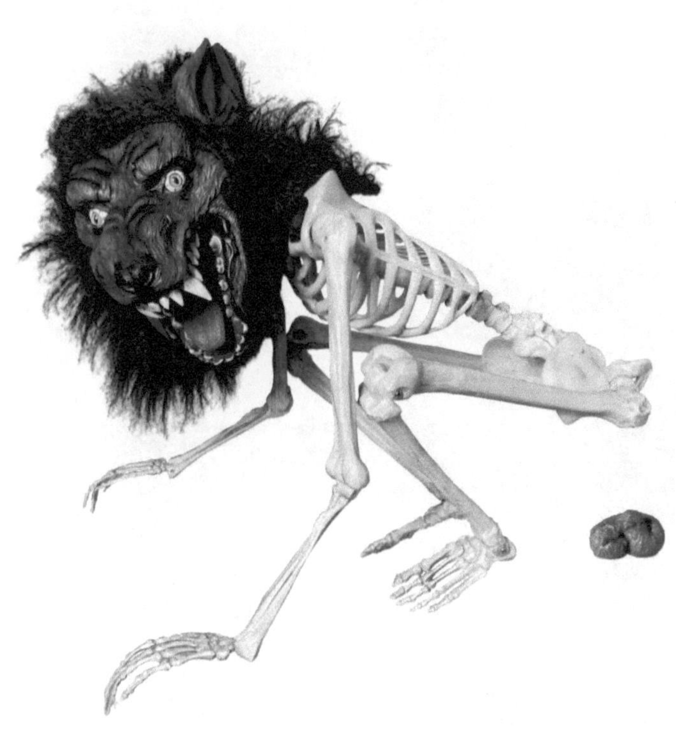

ALSO FROM READ-O-VISION
RISE OF DOCTOR FROWNYFACE
A summer of sex, drugs, and partying by a group of horny young friends ends before it begins when a mad scientist blackmails a perverted mayor, addicts a small town to zombifying drugs, and unleashes a deadly super-virus.
QUEASY! SLEAZY! CHEESY!

18+
"Dusty Trice . . . has a deadly wit."
-Roger Ebert
RISE OF
DOCTOR
FROWNYFACE
THE EROTIC
SCI-FI HORROR
THRILLER BY DUSTY TRICE
BASED ON THE SCREENPLAY
BY DUSTY TRICE AND DR. BRIAN
BASED ON AN ORIGINAL
AND CHARACTERS BY DUSTY
SEX! DRUGS! VIOLENCE! FORCED ABORTIONS! BIKER GANGS! A DEADLY SUPER-VI...

www.ingramcontent.com/pod-product-compliance
Lightning Source LLC
Chambersburg PA
CBHW020117310726
48970CB00002B/671